DEAD GROUND

Harbinger P.I. Book 4

ADAM J. WRIGHT

Dead Ground

THE HARBINGER P.I. SERIES

LOST SOUL
BURIED MEMORY
DARK MAGIC
DEAD GROUND

CHAPTER 1

L<small>EON, KEEP THE CAR STEADY</small>! I can't get a clear shot!" I was leaning out the passenger side window of Leon's Porsche Cayman, pistol crossbow in hand, while he raced toward the car in front of us. Leon's Porsche had enough horsepower to catch the Buick Regal but this stretch of highway curved around the lake and every time I got a bead on the Buick, Leon over-steered and sent the Cayman drifting over the center line, spoiling my aim.

I slipped back in through the window. "If you're going to buy expensive cars, at least learn how to drive them."

"I'm still getting used to the steering, man. Give me a break."

"A break? When I asked you to come and help me on a stakeout, what made you think bringing a canary-yellow Porsche would be a good idea?"

1

"I thought we might need the speed if the perps made a run for it. And I was right. " He got the car straightened up and hit the gas. The silver Regal loomed large in the windshield, sunlight glinting off its rear window.

"They're not perps, they're demons," I said as I leaned out through the window again. "This isn't a cop show." The sudden rush of air snatched my words away.

"You sure about that?" Leon asked. "I've seen this scene in a hundred different shows on TV."

He was right. This might not be a cop show, yet here I was leaning out of a speeding car while trying to shoot out the tires of the car in front. Sure, I was using a crossbow and enchanted bolts instead of a gun but the concept was the same.

In a way, I was a cop of the preternatural world. I was certainly one of the good guys, anyway.

Sheriff Cantrell, who'd lost two deputies to a frog-eyed monster a couple of weeks ago, would disagree. As far as he was concerned, I was a menace, even though I'd solved a three-year-old cold case for his department, discovered how his wife had been killed, and saved the world from being invaded by a bunch of dark gods.

I took aim at the Regal's rear tire and pulled the crossbow's trigger. The bolt flew into the tire and, because it was enchanted and not an ordinary crossbow bolt, went right through the wheel and came out the other side.

It probably embedded itself into the road but I didn't see that because I had to get back inside the car quickly when we hit a sharp left turn and Leon wrenched the wheel to stop us from hitting the safety railing.

The Regal was out of control. It slammed into the railing and bounced back into the middle of the road. The driver must have slammed on the brakes—or what was left of them—and overcorrected his steering, because the vehicle fishtailed in a cloud of white smoke. The remaining three tires screeched on the asphalt and a smell of burning rubber filled the air.

Then the car accelerated and shot forward again. Only this time, instead of trying to outrun us, the driver seemed to think he could escape by making a sudden turn onto one of the side roads that led to the lake.

"Don't lose them," I told Leon. "They'll probably ditch the car and make a run for it when they get to the trees."

"I won't lose them," he said calmly, his face a mask of grim determination.

The woods by the lake stretched for miles in both directions. If the demons abandoned the Regal and made a run for it, we had to stop them quickly, before we lost them amid the trees.

The car ahead of us skidded to a halt and the front doors on either side opened. A dark figure fled out of each side, one heading for the trees on the right, the other running left.

Leon pressed on the brakes and the Porsche skidded to a stop inches from the Regal's rear bumper. "You go right," I told him, opening my door and chasing the demon that had run into the trees on the left.

I could hear my prey ahead, its feet rustling through the undergrowth, but I couldn't see it. Damn thing was moving fast. I picked up my pace, pumping my arms and legs, being careful to avoid roots and branches on the ground. If I tripped and fell, the demon would be gone and my week of surveillance would have been wasted.

This morning, I'd received a call from a guy named Bud Clark who ran the Society of Shadows' Salem office. Apparently, he was trying to track down a couple of demons that had killed a Massachusetts investigator. Bud had reason to believe that the demons in question were moving north, through Maine, and he had asked me to be on the lookout. He said they were driving a silver Buick Regal and gave me the license number.

His call came at a time when I had nothing better to do than follow the lead he'd given me. After the cases involving the church at Clara and the monster in the lake, the office had been quiet.

Felicity had had to fly over to Sussex to visit her parents after her mother called her late one night in a panicked state. Felicity's father had suffered a heart attack and was in the hospital. Felicity called me after she arrived back in England to tell me that her father was doing okay but she wanted to stay there a little longer just to make sure and to help her mother. I told her to take all the time she needed and not to worry about work.

The truth was, work was nonexistent. I arrived at the empty office every day and sat around drinking coffee and researching ancient Egyptian magic. I was hoping to find something that might free my friend Mallory from a curse she had become afflicted with after destroying the heart of a sorceress that an Egyptian priest named Rekhmire had bound magically into a box thousands of years ago. Now, Mallory only had one year to live before the curse killed her.

Despite calling Mallory at least a dozen times, and leaving eight or nine voicemails on her phone, I hadn't spoken to her since the night of the Oak House Slaughter, a massacre that had taken place a couple of weeks ago, when the killer known as Mister Scary had killed twenty-two high school students in an abandoned house in Michigan, leaving a single female survivor, Leah Carlyle. Like Mallory, Leah was now being called a Final Girl by the media.

With Felicity gone, Mallory unreachable, and no case to investigate, I was spinning my wheels. The research into ancient curses was leading to a bunch of dead ends.

So when Bud's call came, I was ready to take any opportunity that meant I could escape the four walls of my office. Demon-hunting sounded ideal.

I planned to take my Land Rover, which was back from the shop, down to the highway and sit there for a while, waiting for the Regal to pass by. Then, I'd follow it until it pulled over somewhere and I would deal with its demonic occupants quickly and quietly.

Before I left the office, though, I decided I owed Leon some action. He and his butler, Michael, had helped out with the lake monster case and Leon was always asking me if he could get involved in any other work, big or small. So I called him and told him I was staking out the highway and asked if he'd like to help. I warned him it would probably mean hours of sitting at the roadside and being bored. But if he wanted to, he could drive.

He jumped at the opportunity. And turned up in a canary-yellow Porsche Cayman.

As it turned out, we only had to wait an hour before the Regal went rolling by. But as soon as Leon pulled out into the road, the demons must have sensed they were being followed because they went hell for leather.

So now here I was, searching for one of them in the woods while Leon chased its companion.

I saw movement ahead and raised the pistol crossbow. But before I could release a bolt, the demon dodged behind the trees. I ran on, following the sound of its feet disturbing the undergrowth and snapping twigs. When I saw it again, it was fifty yards ahead of me and increasing that distance fast.

I stopped and aimed the pistol crossbow with both hands, trying to remain calm and not rush the shot. When I finally released the bolt, it flew between the trees and caught the demon's right shoulder blade. The creature stumbled and fell. The bolt I'd just shot it with was specifically enchanted to take down demonic beings. The magic that was bound to the projectile was like napalm when it hit its intended target.

The demon hissed in pain and tried to get back to its feet. I rushed toward it, reloading the crossbow. I had an enchanted dagger fixed to my belt but I was hoping I wouldn't need to get that close to the creature.

As I approached the demon, I saw it clearly for the first time. It was tall and heavily-built, like a six-and-a-half-foot linebacker. Its skin was scaly and the color of old, dried blood. When its eyes glared at me, they were bright yellow and snake-like. It reached back and tore the crossbow bolt from its shoulder. Staggering to its feet, it sneered at me. "Another investigator. I will deal with you just as I dealt with the investigator in Salem."

"Yeah, I don't think so," I said. "I'm the one holding the crossbow and you're the one covered in dirt."

It laughed, a hideous sound that made me feel cold inside. "You have no idea what is coming, investigator. Your puny Society of Shadows shall be crushed beneath the might of the Midnight Cabal."

"Oh, you're with those guys, huh?" I'd heard about the rise of the Cabal from my father. Apparently, they were a group as old as the Society but instead of wanting to save the world, they wanted to throw it back into the superstitious chaos of the Middle Ages.

The demon sneered again. "One day, this world shall belong to our kind."

"Is that right? Well, unfortunately for you, you won't be around to see it. Bye." I shot it through the heart with an enchanted bolt. The demon shrieked and collapsed to the ground, the hateful yellow light in its eyes dimming. When the lights went out entirely, the body began to disintegrate into ash.

I retraced my steps to the cars and then quickly crossed over the road to the section of the woods where the other demon had fled. I'd given Leon shotgun shells enchanted with the demon napalm magic but I still hurried through the trees. These creatures were dangerous.

A couple of seconds after I'd entered this part of the woods, I heard a shotgun blast, then another. I ran toward the sound and found Leon standing over a pile of ash.

"Hey," I said as nonchalantly as I could. I didn't want Leon to think that I'd been worried about him. He enjoyed this and he was good at it and I didn't want to shake his confidence in any way.

He gave me a little wave. He was sweating and breathing heavily from chasing down the demon that now lay dead—well, disintegrated—at his feet.

"Good job," I said.

"No problem at all," he said, grinning. "We should do this more often. That was fun."

We started to walk back through the trees toward the cars. "Thanks for your help," I said. "I'll call Bud Clark and tell him we got his demons. Want to grab a bite to eat at Darla's?"

"Yeah, sounds good."

When we reached the cars, Leon asked, "How come you brought me on this job and not Felicity? I thought you two were inseparable."

"She's in England at the moment," I said, putting the pistol crossbow into the Porsche's trunk. "Her dad had a heart attack so she's gone over there to be with her family."

"Oh, I'm sorry to hear that, man." He got into the driver's seat.

I closed the trunk and slid into the passenger seat. "She should be back soon."

Leon grinned and looked at me knowingly.

"What?" I asked him.

"Nothing. It's just that I've seen you two together and I think maybe there's more there than just a working relationship, if you know what I mean?"

"Yeah, I know exactly what you mean. Now get us to Darla's."

He started the engine. It roared to life and then settled into a smooth purr. "You don't want to talk about it?"

I shook my head. "I don't want to talk about it."

Leon shrugged and turned the Porsche around. When we got to the highway, he said, "I just meant it would be cool if you two were a thing. Felicity is intelligent and she can kick ass when she needs to. And, of course, she's smoking hot."

I really didn't want to have this conversation with Leon. He was right about Felicity—she was all those things and more—but our relationship had only taken tiny steps beyond being purely professional. Neither of us was sure what was happening or where it was going to lead. And now that she was in England, it was leading nowhere.

I missed her, and that was nothing to do with work. She was an amazing assistant, and an invaluable resource when it came to occult languages and symbols, but I missed just having her around. She was funny and smart and caring, a good person who was willing to step into the fight against evil and give it her all. I missed talking to her and getting her input on cases.

Of course, at the moment, there were no cases. After eating a burger with Leon, I'd be returning to an empty office and more unproductive hours researching ancient Egyptian magic. I'd probably do the Midnight Cabal a favor and die of boredom.

"Where's Michael today?" I asked Leon, hoping to shut down his line of inquiry regarding Felicity. Leon was rarely seen without his butler. In fact, I'd never seen one without the other.

"It's his summer vacation. He usually tends to the plants in his hothouse during his free time. He grows orchids and that kind of thing. And he talks to them. Says its makes them grow faster."

"Really?" I tried to visualize Michael talking to orchids in a hothouse. It was difficult to reconcile with what I had seen of the man. He was tough and courageous, more like Leon's bodyguard than his butler.

Leon chuckled. "Yeah, I know. That doesn't sound like Michael, right? He says it relaxes him. He used to be a soldier and I think growing flowers helps him forget about some of the things he's seen."

"That makes sense," I said. I could imagine Michael in the army, probably as a member of a Special Forces unit.

We got to Darla's Diner and Leon found a space in the corner of the parking lot. As usual, Darla's was busy. I could see through the windows that most of the booths and tables were occupied by customers. It was one of the best places to eat in the area and was frequented by locals as well as truckers passing through on their way to New Hampshire, Massachusetts, and New York.

Inside, the air was cool thanks to the AC. There was a smell of fried meat and onions that I was sure got pumped out of the vents along with the air to make the customers hungrier. Leon slid quickly into a booth by the window that had just been vacated by a group of truckers. I sat opposite him.

"Are you paying for this?" he asked as he inspected his menu.

I laughed. "I thought you made millions from those apps you developed?"

He looked at me over the top of the menu, his brown eyes humorous. "I do. But I demand some form of payment for chasing down those demons."

"You demand payment, huh? You sound like that faerie queen who made me pledge my services to her."

His expression turned suddenly serious. "Did anything ever come of that? What did she want you to do?"

I shrugged. "Nothing yet. I guess I'll hear from her when she wants something." Leon and I had been lost in the realm of Faerie and I'd had to agree to be of service to the Lady of the Forest in exchange for a way back home.

The terms I'd agreed to meant I could refuse any request but until I accepted one, I was indebted to the Lady. As far as deals with the fae went, it wasn't all that bad but I didn't like being indebted to anyone, never mind a faerie queen.

"That was a crazy place," Leon said.

"Crazy and dangerous. It isn't on my list of favorite places to visit."

The waitress, a young dark-haired girl, came over and cleared the table. "I'll take your orders in a moment," she said before she left with the dirty dishes.

Leon flashed her a smile and then turned his attention back to me. "You got any more jobs lined up that I can help you with?"

I shook my head. "I haven't got any jobs lined up at all. Business hasn't exactly been booming lately."

"That's a shame." His face fell for a moment but then lifted into an easy smile when the waitress returned.

"What can I get you?" she asked.

I ordered a Darla's Double Burger and Coke. Leon ordered the same. The waitress filled our coffee cups and disappeared.

"So what are you going to do?" Leon asked me.

"I don't know. Wait for something to turn up, I guess."

He nodded. "I get bored easily. That's why I still work on new apps and stuff even though I don't need the money anymore. I tried to retire once but I felt like I was going crazy after a couple of weeks so I went right back to creating apps."

"Well, my job doesn't work like that. I can't create a monster to hunt or a case to investigate. I have to wait for them to turn up."

"Yeah, that sucks." He gestured out the window to the yellow Porsche Cayman. "That's why I buy stuff, you know. Because I get bored."

I nodded. "Yeah, I kinda figured that."

"It works for a while but then I get bored of whatever it was I bought. Like, the cars are fun and all, but eventually that Porsche will just join the others in the garage."

"You need to get a hobby," I told him. "Like Michael's orchids."

Leon shrugged. "Playing around with computers was my hobby until I started making money at it. Then, I worked for so many hours on the apps that eventually I got sick of it. But I can't just sit around on my ass all day either. I have to be doing something. You have the perfect job. It's always different and exciting."

"It isn't all about sticking swords into monsters and demons," I said. "There's research and paperwork too."

He looked unconvinced. "Every time I see you, you're slaying something with that kickass sword. That's why I said you're like a modern-day knight. You're slaying dragons most of the time."

I shrugged. Maybe he was right. Besides, Felicity handled most of the paperwork because she enjoyed it. That left me to do the physical work. The perfect team.

The waitress brought our burgers and Cokes to the table and set them in front of us. "Anything else you need, just let me know," she said with a smile before heading over to serve a family at a nearby table.

My phone buzzed in my pocket. I ignored it while I took a bite of the juicy burger. As usual, it melted in my mouth and flooded my taste buds with delicious flavor.

"Best burger around," Leon said.

I nodded and fished my phone from my pocket. The screen displayed the name *Jim Walker*.

I hadn't heard from Jim in maybe six months. He was the investigator I'd worked with in Canada while trying to log my year's worth of field experience and become a fully-fledged investigator.

Jim had been a great mentor and, as well as teaching me the business of investigating the preternatural, he had also taught me some nature spells that had been passed down by his First Nations ancestors. I'd used one of those spells at Dearmont Lake when I'd asked the trees to reveal the details of Deirdre Summers' death.

I answered the call. "Hey, Jim."

"Hey, Alec. How's it going in the Windy City?"

"I'm not in Chicago anymore," I said. "I got reassigned to a little place in Maine."

"What? How did that happen?"

"It's a long story."

"Okay, no need to go into it right now. I was wondering if you'd like to come up north for a few days? I'd sure like to see you."

"You have a problem?" I asked.

"Yeah, maybe."

"What is it?"

"I'm not really sure. It's a mystery. There have been some weird murders. The police don't know what's happening and, frankly, neither do I. My crystals aren't detecting any magic at the crime scenes but there's something strange going on. So I thought I'd call you. Maybe a fresh pair of eyes would be good. You've worked this area before and it's too long since we've seen each other. We can have a few beers and you can tell me that long story."

"Sounds good, Jim. I'll arrange a flight to Toronto. It'll probably be tomorrow."

"That soon?" he asked, surprise in his voice. "I thought you'd have to close your current cases first. I wasn't expecting you until sometime next week."

"My schedule is clear right now," I said.

"The town is that small?"

"Yeah, you could say that. So, tell me about the murders."

Leon leaned forward over the table. "If it's a new case, I want to help."

"Who's that?" Jim asked.

"Someone I've been working with."

"Is he any good?"

I thought of Leon standing over the pile of ash that had once been a demon. "Yeah, he's good."

Leon beamed.

"Bring him along, if you want," Jim said.

"I'll think about it. So…the murders?"

"Oh, yeah. I'll let you see for yourself when you get here."

"Okay," I said, intrigued. "I'll see you sometime tomorrow." I ended the call and went back to eating my burger.

Leon looked like he was about to burst with excitement. "Well? Who was that? Do we have another case?"

"I have another case," I said.

"But you're taking me along, right?"

I sighed. Leon was my friend and I didn't want to put him in any danger, even though I'd done so on numerous occasions already. "It doesn't sound exciting enough for you," I said. "It's a murder investigation."

He looked at me closely to see if I was joking. "Are you kidding? Dude, I've seen every episode of C.S.I. I love murder investigations." Then he narrowed his eyes. "Wait a minute, this can't be a normal murder case or the police would be handling it. There has to be something weird about it for you to get involved."

"Yeah, there is."

He leaned forward and looked around the diner as if we might be being watched. "What is it?" he whispered conspiratorially. "Demons? Vampires?"

"I gave no idea," I said, taking another bite of my burger. "My friend Jim is going to tell me when I get there."

Leon frowned. "You mean he's going to tell *us* when *we* get there, right?"

I considered it while I ate more of the burger. I didn't mind taking Leon on the case just as long as the something weird didn't turn into something dangerous. I didn't want to be responsible for putting him in harm's way. But who was I kidding? I'd put Leon in danger on more than one occasion and he'd come through each time. I was doing him a disservice by thinking he couldn't handle himself.

Besides, the case Jim was talking about didn't sound too risky. Investigating a few murders—weird or not—wasn't as dangerous as fighting the monster we'd faced at the lake.

"You're really bored, aren't you?" I asked Leon.

He nodded. "I don't like summer, man. My friends have a few parties and things but it just isn't exciting. So I spend most of my time locked away, playing games. I hardly ever see the sun. If I were a white guy, I'd be pasty right now. You should take me with you for the sake of my health, if nothing else. I need to be outdoors."

I grinned. "Okay, you're in. I can't let you waste away in front of your computer. I just hope you can handle the wilderness."

"The wilderness? Where are we going?"

I finished my burger and pushed the plate away. "We're going to Canada."

CHAPTER 2

At 4:50 P.M. THE FOLLOWING day, Leon and I were in Huntsville, Ontario, both of us leaning on the dark blue Ford Explorer I'd rented. The Explorer was parked on Main Street, right outside the door of Jim's office. The door was locked, so Leon and I were just hanging around, waiting.

It had been a long day, beginning with a 6:00 a.m. flight from Bangor, and I was tired. Standing with my hands in my pockets, I stared up at the sky, which was bright and cloudless. Leon was playing with his phone, concentrating on the screen.

"I thought you wanted to get away from all that?" I said.

"Huh?" He looked up at me.

I nodded at his phone. "I thought you wanted to escape the machines and get back to nature?"

"No, I never said that. I said I needed to get outdoors." He gestured at the street. "As you can see, I'm outdoors."

"Well, you should probably make the most of your phone now because there might not be any coverage where we're going."

He looked shocked. "What? When you told me we were coming to Canada, you didn't mention we were leaving civilization behind."

"All I'm saying is that a lot of Jim's work is done in Algonquin Park. There's cell coverage along the highway that runs through the park but there isn't any in the backcountry. If we need to spend time in the places away from the main road, your phone won't work there."

He sighed. "How big is this park anyway?"

"Three thousand square miles of lakes and forest. It's larger than Delaware."

Leon raised his eyebrows. "How are we supposed to find a monster in all that? And how do we even know what we're looking for?"

"There are usually things called clues," I said sarcastically.

He shot me a look that told me to stop being a smartass.

"Besides, Jim is an expert tracker," I told him. "He taught me a few things too."

"So this guy was, like, your mentor or something?"

"Exactly. When I came to work with Jim, everything I knew about being an investigator was purely academic. The only preternatural creatures I'd seen were in the classroom, in photos and videos. Working with Jim brought all that learning into practice. It all became real. And I loved it. Jim taught me the little tricks and tips he'd picked up from working in the field for years."

"So he's an old dude," Leon said.

"Hey, I'm not old," came a voice from the street. A black Jeep Renegade had stopped on the road and Jim Walker was leaning out of the open driver's window, a grin on his face.

He didn't look any older than he had the last time I'd seen him. His dark brown eyes shone with energy, and his face, framed by long straight black hair, was well-defined with strong cheekbones and chin. Jim was in his fifties but I knew he could outrun and outfight men half his age.

Oblivious to the traffic stopped behind his Jeep, Jim got out and came over to me, arms wide. He wore boots, blue jeans, and a black T-shirt that was tight on his heavily-muscled frame and showed off the tribal tattoos on his huge arms. Jim had added them to his Society tattoos and was covered in ink from the base of his neck to his ankles.

He caught me in a hug that could crush a grizzly. "Alec, it's good to see you."

"You too, Jim," I managed, despite the air being squeezed from my lungs. "This is Leon Smith, a friend of mine."

"And now mine," Jim said, pumping Leon's hand. When he released it, Leon rubbed his fingers gingerly.

Jim went back to the Renegade. "Come on, there's been another murder. The police called me a few moments ago."

"Is it in the park?" I asked, opening the Explorer.

Jim got into his vehicle and nodded. "Yeah, the park. That's where it's all happening."

Leon got into the passenger seat, still rubbing his hand. I turned to him and smiled. "We're going to the park."

"Yeah, so I hear." He opened the Explorer's glove compartment, sighed, and threw his phone into it.

CHAPTER 3

I FOLLOWED JIM OUT OF Huntsville and along Highway 60. When we got to Algonquin's West Gate, I had to pay to get a permit to enter the park. The girl who sold it to me said that if I was just driving through and didn't intend to stop anywhere in the park, I didn't need it. I told her that I did indeed intend to stop but didn't mention I would be to examining a murder scene.

With the permit sitting on the Explorer's dash, I followed Jim's Jeep along the highway for maybe twenty miles until he pulled into a parking area at the side of road. I did the same and cut the engine. There were two black-and-white police cruisers parked here, as well as a dark green Chevy Tahoe and a blue Honda Civic. There were no police officers in sight.

Leon and I got out of the Explorer and Jim came over to us. "The crime scene is a couple of miles along this trail," he said, pointing at a dirt trail that led into the trees. "It was discovered by a hiker a couple of hours ago."

"What equipment do we need?" I asked.

"It's all in here." He showed me a small black backpack. "Crystal shards and faerie stones. But like I told you before, I'm not detecting magic at any of these scenes."

We set off into the woods. The warm evening air swarmed with insects that bothered Leon and me but seemed to leave Jim alone. He watched as we swatted at the bugs that attacked us, and chuckled. "You guys need to learn that bug repellent is your friend."

"I didn't realize we'd be coming out into the woods so soon," I said, waving my hand at a mosquito that buzzed near my ear.

"Do the police call you every time they get a murder?" Leon asked Jim.

"Only when there's something they can't explain," Jim said. "They got me to consult on this case when they found the first body a couple of weeks ago. A second body turned up a week later and the police decided to keep me on the case."

"What's so strange about the bodies?" I asked, wishing that my relationship with the police in Dearmont could be as good as Jim's was with the Ontario Provincial Police. Instead of being hated by local law enforcement, Jim was

24

respected and was called on whenever a non-mundane perspective could help solve a case. And, as more cases had been solved with Jim's help, his reputation as a valuable asset to the O.P.P. had grown.

"It's always a lone victim and the attacks happen at night. The bodies are torn up and have been fed on," Jim said. "But the tears and bite marks don't match any known animal."

"Werewolves?" I asked.

Jim shook his head. "When I say any known animal, I'm including all the ones known to me as well as the police. I did some research on the Society database but there's a lot of information on there regarding creatures that tear their victims apart. I can't narrow it down."

"It's a shame we don't have Felicity here," I said. "She's really good at this kind of thing."

"Who's Felicity?" Jim asked.

"My assistant."

"Assistant? You're really coming up in the world, my friend. The only assistant I ever had was you and you weren't really good at anything." He grinned.

"Really?" I said. "I seem to remember saving your ass from a wendigo that was about to make you its lunch."

He shrugged. "I might have gotten away before it had a chance to chow down on me."

"Yeah, I don't think so." I said to Leon, "Jim might look big and strong but he'd been pumped so full of wendigo poison that I had to drag him out of the woods."

"It wasn't far," Jim said.

"At least three miles," I told Leon.

Leon laughed. "Sounds like you two had some good times."

Jim clapped him on the shoulder. "We did, but don't believe anything Alec tells you about them. He'll try to make it sound like he was the hero but I was protecting him every step of the way."

"So you were protecting me when we went into that nest of vampires in North Bay and you were knocked unconscious the minute we got through the door?" I said to Leon, "I had to kill them all myself and then drag Jim back to the car."

Jim sighed. "You're giving Leon the wrong idea. It sounds like you spent all your time dragging me around."

I thought for a moment. "Oh, and there was that time we faced a pack of werewolves—"

"Don't listen to him, Leon," Jim said, cutting me off. "He's skipping over all the times I saved his ass. There are so many of those, I don't even know where to begin."

I laughed. "Okay, Jim, let's concede that we saved each other more times that we can remember."

"You guys have the best job in the world," Leon said.

"It isn't all fun and games," Jim said, his tone growing more serious. "We look back at those moments and laugh but only because to take it seriously would lead to a mental breakdown. People get hurt and killed by the monsters we hunt. Sometimes, we have to face things we'd rather not see. Laugher is the only way to make the mental scars a little less deep."

"Case in point," I said, pointing to where four police officers were searching the ground and undergrowth around the trail. There was a purple-and-white tent in a small clearing. It had been ripped apart, the fabric hanging raggedly from the metal frame like flesh torn from bone.

The four police officers—three men and a woman—turned to us as we approached. Jim waved and asked, "Same as last time?"

"Looks like it," the female police officer said. "The body—what's left of it—is in the tent."

"Where are Frasier and Girard?" Jim asked.

She pointed at the trees beyond the tent. "Over there, searching for clues."

"Mind if we take a look at the body?"

She looked at Leon and me before shrugging. "Sure."

We followed Jim to the tent. The smell of dead flesh hung in the warm summer air. The body lying inside the ruined tent was male, maybe in his late twenties, with messy dark hair and a beard. He was lying on his back and was naked except for a pair of blue boxers. His chest had been ripped open, the ribs parted to allow access to the internal organs.

"Same as the others," Jim said. "When the M.E. examines the body, she'll find that most of his organs are gone."

"That's gross, man," Leon said. He wasn't looking at the body; he was staring at the fat flies buzzing around it and crawling over the remnants of the tent.

"I don't think it was a lone victim this time," I said. "There were two people in here." The shredded remains of a dark blue sleeping bag lay around the body and still covered the lower parts of his legs. A dark green sleeping bag was next to him. The green bag was intact and had been unzipped.

I looked at the torn pieces of tent lying around until I found the tent's door flap. Like the green sleeping bag, it was unzipped. "Looks like the second person fled the tent while this guy was being torn apart."

"It was a woman," Jim said, pointing to a jumble of female clothing in one corner of the tent.

I looked at the dense forest around us. "So where is she?"

Jim inspected the grass and natural debris on the ground. He pointed along the trail. "She went that way."

"She was running, so she should be easy enough to track," I said.

Jim nodded. "Yeah, should be." He walked the trail slowly, his eyes locked on the ground, looking for signs like broken twigs, depressions in the dirt, and scattered leaves. "She came this way."

Leon looked at the trail ahead and then back the way we had come. "It doesn't make sense. Why would she run this way instead of back to the main road?"

"She was panicking," Jim said. "And the fact that they were in their sleeping bags indicates the attack took place last night. She was running in the darkness, confused and terrified. He pointed at an area of grass at the edge of the trail. "She fell here." He inspected the ground around the area. "And then she disappeared."

"What?" Leon asked.

"She didn't go any farther than this. She fell over here, probably tripping over a tree root or branch, and then vanished. There are no more signs."

I examined the trail. "And there are no signs that anything was following her."

"No," Jim confirmed. "It's like she was running from a ghost."

"Whatever killed that guy wasn't a ghost," I said.

Jim opened the backpack and took out a crystal shard. He held it up so we could see that it wasn't glowing. "It wasn't a magical creature or some kind of spell either. There's no trace of magic here at all."

"So something broke into the tent but left no tracks," I said. "It ripped the guy open and fed on him while the woman got out of the tent and ran along the trail. She fell here and then there's no further trace of her or the thing that took her."

Jim stroked his chin, looking along the trail and then back to where the police officers searched the undergrowth. Then his gaze turned slowly upward to the evening sky.

When he did that, I knew what he was thinking. "It can fly," I said.

Jim nodded. "It plucked the woman off the ground and took her to its lair."

Leon was also looking up at the sky. "So what the hell is it?"

"A nightwing," Jim said.

"Sounds like you guys have been reading too many comic books." The voice brought my attention back to the trail where a man in a gray sports jacket, gray tie, and black pants was walking toward us from the clearing. He was bald, sported a goatee, and wore shades. He was lean and tough-looking.

"Detective Girard," Jim whispered to us.

Behind the bald detective, walking briskly to catch up with him, was a petite redhead in a gray pantsuit. She also wore shades. "We don't have time for this, Girard," she said.

"Don't have time?" he asked sarcastically. "But Walker was about to reveal the murderer. I'm sure he said we should be on the lookout for Nightwing. I'm beginning to think he doesn't know the difference between fantasy and reality. Oh, yeah, that's right, he doesn't"

She shook her head at him. I was sure she was rolling her eyes behind the shades.

"Who are your friends?" Girard asked Walker when he reached us. "No, wait, don't tell me. These guys are elves who came from Mordor to help you solve the case."

"Elves don't live in Mordor," Leon said.

Girard looked at him for a moment before saying, "Is that right?"

The woman's manner was friendlier. She removed her shades to reveal bright blue eyes, and said, "Hi, I'm Detective Frasier and this is my partner Detective Girard." She held out her hand to Leon, and then, after shaking with him, did the same with me. Her grip was strong, despite her small frame.

Girard kept his hands firmly in his pockets.

"What have you got for us?" Frasier asked Jim.

"There were two victims this time," Jim told her.

"Yeah," she said. "The guy in the tent is Michael Roland, twenty-four, from Quebec. His girlfriend, Jeanette Gautier, twenty-two, also from Quebec, is missing. She held up two driver's licenses. One showed the dark-haired guy from the tent on a decidedly better day. The other showed a young blond woman whom I hoped was still alive.

"She's been taken," Jim said. "The creature descended on the tent, ripped it apart and got inside. While it was making a meal of Roland, the woman got out of there and fled along the trail to this spot, where she fell. When it was finished eating, the creature swooped along the trail and lifted her into the air."

"Holy shit, is she still alive?" Frasier asked.

"I doubt it," Jim said grimly.

31

Girard snorted. "Don't tell me you believe this bullshit, Claire."

She narrowed her bright blue eyes and shot him a look. Turning her attention back to Jim and letting the angry look fade, she asked, "How do we find this thing and kill it?"

"We need to find its lair. It'll be a cave or a secluded area where it can sleep undisturbed during the day. A place that is hidden from the sun. These creatures are nocturnal; their eyes are adapted to darkness and can't tolerate daylight."

Girard threw up his hands in frustration. "I can't believe we're listening to this. We should be focusing on what really happened here. These people were attacked by a bear, not by a winged monster from a fairytale."

"The M.E. doesn't recognize the bite or claw marks," Frasier reminded him.

"So we need to get a second opinion. That tent back there and the poor guy inside it were ripped apart by a bear. The girl got away and is wandering around in the woods somewhere. We need to look at the evidence in front of our faces instead of listening to this guy," he pointed at Jim, "and becoming the laughing stock of the department."

"If it was a bear," Jim said calmly, "where are the tracks? There's no evidence that a bear was ever here."

Girard sighed in frustration and turned on his heels. As he started back along the trail, he shouted back at us, "It's a bear. When it turns out I'm right, your police consulting days are over, Walker." He stalked past the officers searching the undergrowth. "When you're ready to do some real police work, Claire, I'll be waiting in the car."

Frasier took a deep breath, as if trying to calm herself. "I'm sorry," she said, looking from Leon, to me, to Jim. "Girard is set in his ways."

"That's one way of putting it," Jim said.

"He's a good detective," she said. "He's just," —she threw up her arms in frustration—"Girard." As if that explained everything.

A radio on her belt beeped. She unclipped it and brought it up to her face. "Frasier."

A female voice on the other end said, "We found the girl. She's a half mile up the trail from your location."

"Alive or dead?" Frasier asked.

"She's dead."

A sadness entered Frasier's eyes and I wondered if she'd thought she could actually save Jeanette Gautier. "Is she in the same state as the guy?" she said into the radio.

"It's difficult to tell. We're going to need some ladders up here."

Frasier frowned. "Ladders? What for?"

There was a pause and then the female officer said, "The body is at the top of a pine tree."

CHAPTER 4

JEANETTE GAUTIER LAY ON HER back, balanced on the uppermost branches of a tall pine tree. The police officer had said it was difficult to tell if Jeanette was in the same state as Michael Roland but I could see torn pieces of flesh hanging from the body. I had no doubt that when they got the ladders up to her, they'd find the ribs pulled open and the internal organs gone.

I looked at Jim. "This is bad."

He nodded. "The creature is marking its territory."

I turned to Frasier, who was staring up at the woman's body. "You need to get everyone out of here by nightfall," I told her. "Tell the park rangers to close off this entire area."

She nodded, concern in her eyes. "Do you think it will come back tonight?"

"It's possible. The creature's feeding pattern seems to be once a week but now that it's started doing this,"—I indicated the body in the tree—"it's marking its territory and becoming more aggressive."

Girard sauntered over to us, hands still in his pockets. Frasier had called him with the news that Jeanette Gautier's body had been found and now Girard looked like he'd been chewing on a sour lemon.

"Still think it's a bear?" Jim asked him.

Girard's expression was unreadable behind his shades. He stared at Jim but said nothing.

I took Jim and Leon to one side and said, "We have more chance of finding this thing now that it's staked a claim to this area. Its lair must be somewhere around here."

Jim nodded. "We can study the maps I have at the house and look for the most likely place the creature is holed up. Then, we can hunt it during daylight tomorrow."

"Sounds like a plan," I said. Nightwings were much easier to kill during the day than at night.

We walked back along the trail to the cars. "Frasier seems open-minded," I said to Jim, "but her partner's an asshole."

"Yeah, grade-A," he said. "Claire is good people, though. I sometimes go fishing with her husband. Nice guy. Claire has seen enough weird stuff that she doesn't dismiss anything out of hand. Girard is stubborn as a mule and has a nasty streak too. He wouldn't admit this was a nightwing attack even if we brought the body to the police station and put it on his desk."

"Is anybody going to tell me what a nightwing is?" Leon asked when we were out of earshot of the police.

"A nightwing isn't a specific creature," I told him. "It's a classification used to describe a winged preternatural being that flies and hunts at night. Within that class, there are many different creatures. Usually, nightwings stay hidden and only feed occasionally so they go unnoticed but every now and then, there are sightings and the media jumps on it. There was a nightwing in West Virginia in the sixties that became known as the Mothman. There were some sightings in Chile a few years ago of a flying monster that was killing cattle at night. Eventually, the creature disappeared, meaning it probably left the area for somewhere more quiet, away from humans.

"The creature that killed Roland and Gautier is much more aggressive than usual. Taking two victims like that and staking its territory isn't typical nightwing behavior."

"Which is why we should find out exactly what we're dealing with," Jim said.

"I guess I could call Felicity," I said. "She can check the database when she gets a chance."

"That would be useful," Jim said.

We reached the cars and I realized how quickly it was getting dark. Back on the trail, I'd assumed some of the gloom was due to being beneath the tree canopy but now that we were back at the road, I could see the sky becoming a deep blue shot through with blood-red streaks.

"Are you guys getting the food?" Jim asked as he opened the door of his Jeep.

"Yeah, sure," I said, climbing into the Explorer. "We'll see you at your place. Get the beers ready." I waited for Leon to get in before I backed out onto the road and followed Jim back to the West Gate and along Highway 60.

Before we reached Huntsville, Jim turned off the highway and headed north toward his home. I drove into town and parked outside a Chinese restaurant.

"I'll get this," Leon said, getting out of the car and going into the restaurant.

I got out and leaned against the Explorer while I called Felicity. The sky was almost fully dark now and I hoped Frasier had gotten everyone off that trail. I'd never heard of a nightwing attacking a large group of people but the creature in the park seemed to be playing by its own rules. And it would be easy for a police officer or EMT crew member to wander away from the others in the darkness and find themselves torn apart by the lurking monster.

The call took a while to connect, probably because it was long distance, and when Felicity finally answered, her voice sounded faint and faraway. "Alec, is that you?"

"Yeah, it's me," I said. "How are you?" I immediately felt guilty for not calling her sooner. I'd wanted to give her some space to deal with her family problems but maybe it would've been better if I'd called at least once to see how she was doing.

"I'm fine," she said. "Things are settling down a bit. Dad has come home from the hospital and Mum and I are fussing around him so much, I think he'll be glad when I leave. I can come back to work whenever you need me. Is that why you're calling? Is there a case?"

"There's a case," I said, "but you don't need to jump on the next plane over here or anything. I'm in Canada, working a case with Jim Walker. Leon's here too."

"Canada? Who's running the office? What if we get some new clients in Dearmont?"

"Don't worry about it. The office phone is forwarded to my cell. Nobody's called and I should only be here for a few days anyway. This case is pretty straightforward. There's a nightwing killing people up here so we're going to find its lair and deal with it."

"A nightwing? What type?"

"We don't know yet. I was wondering if you'd take a look at the Society database and see if you can narrow it down?"

"Of course. What information do you have?" She was in work mode immediately.

"Well, it seems to be feeding once a week, on human internal organs. It's living in a forested area with lakes and rivers. And it's marking its territory by placing the bodies of its victims in trees."

"Was that a male or female victim? And what type of tree was it?"

"Female. And the tree was a red pine."

"All right, I'll look into it."

"Call me if you find anything, no matter what time it is. In fact, I just realized, it must be pretty late there. Did I wake you?"

"It's fine. I'll call you as soon as I find out exactly what you're dealing with."

"Thanks, Felicity."

"And, Alec…" She paused.

"Yeah?" I asked.

"Please be careful."

"Always. I'll talk to you later. Goodnight." I ended the call.

A couple minutes later, Leon came out of the restaurant, laden down with two boxes full of food containers.

"Did you leave any food for the other customers?" I asked him, taking one of the boxes and putting it into the back of the Explorer.

"I wasn't sure what everyone likes so I got some of everything," he said.

"Well, it smells good," I told him. The last thing I'd eaten was a small bag of dill pickle potato chips in Toronto and that had been hours ago.

As we took the highway out of Huntsville and then got onto the road that led to Jim's house, I looked out of the windshield at the dark trees in the distance.

Somewhere out there was a monster. If we didn't stop it, it would take more innocent lives.

I couldn't allow that to happen.

CHAPTER 5

Jim's house was north of Huntsville, close to Arrowhead Provincial Park, and situated on a small lake where Jim and I had spent many hours fishing from his canoe and swimming out to the wooden raft floating fifty feet from the shore. We used to spend hours sitting in the sun by the lake and talking about our cases.

The house was rustic-looking, built in the Adirondack style from wood and stone, with rugged tree trunks used as the support pillars for the porch that overlooked the lake. Built on the expanse of grass that led down to the water was a Muskoka granite barbecue that Jim used to cook almost all his meals during the spring and summer months. We'd discussed many cases in front of that barbecue, drinking beer and figuring out how to save the world from some nasty or other, while burgers sizzled on the grill.

"Nice place," Leon said as I parked next to Jim's Jeep at the side of the house. "A little rustic, maybe."

"Leon, you live in an ultra-modern mansion made of steel and glass. The Sydney Opera House probably looks rustic to you."

We got out of the car and took a box each of the Chinese food out of the back before carrying them across the grass and setting them down on the picnic table by the barbecue.

Then we went back to the car and took out our cases, setting them down on the deck.

"Hey, I thought you guys would never get here." Jim came out of the house with a white plastic cooler and placed it on the ground next to the table.

"Leon bought the entire menu," I told Jim.

"Not quite," Leon said. "I got a variety of things because I didn't know what you guys like."

"If it's food, I like it," Jim said, inspecting the contents of the cardboard boxes. "I'll get some plates." He disappeared back into the house and returned a few seconds later with plates, dishes, forks, and chopsticks wrapped in paper packets.

We unloaded the boxes and took a plate each, loading them with whatever looked and smelled good. Everything looked and smelled good so my plate ended up being piled high with chicken chop suey, fried rice, sweet and sour chicken, and Szechuan pork. I unwrapped a set of chopsticks, wondering what to taste first.

Jim took three bottles of Molson Canadian from the cooler and handed them out. The ice-cold bottles were covered in droplets of condensation.

When we were done eating and Jim had squirreled away the leftovers into his fridge, he brought out a map of the area and laid it on the table. Two small circles had been drawn on the map in red marker and now Jim added a third on the trail where we had found Michael Roland and Jeanette Gautier.

I noticed a pattern immediately. "It's moving closer to the highway. The first kill was deeper in the woods, the second a little closer to the main road, and the third even closer."

Jim nodded. "It's getting bolder. This isn't the usual behavior of a nightwing. It doesn't make sense."

"Could somebody be controlling it?" I asked, thinking out loud.

"If it was being controlled by magic, the crystal shard would have detected something," Jim said.

Using my finger, I traced a line from the most recent red circle, back to the one from a week ago, and back to the scene of the first murder. From there, I continued in the same direction until I hit a place on the map that was heavily-wooded, with a small lake nearby, and far away from the hiking trails. "What's this area like?" I asked Jim.

"Dense forest, rocky bluffs, a lake, and not much else," he said.

"Typical nightwing territory," I suggested.

ADAM J. WRIGHT

He nodded. "Yeah, that could be where the lair is. It's far enough from the trails that the nightwing could have lived there for years without being seen."

"Not being seen is what these creatures are usually good at," I mused, checking the distance on the map from the remote area to the highway. "So why is it taking prey thirty or forty miles from its home? And why did it put Jeanette Gautier's body in a tree here,"—I pointed at the red circle—"if its territory is all the way over here?" I returned my finger to the remote area.

"Maybe it's expanding its territory," Leon suggested.

I shrugged. "That's a pretty big territory for a nightwing. They usually stick close to their lairs."

Jim pointed at the remote forest and small lake. "We'll check out this area early tomorrow morning so we can make use of as much daylight as possible."

"Agreed," I said.

Jim folded the map and picked up the cooler of beers. "Now, come and sit on the porch and tell me how the hell you ended up getting kicked out of Chicago and sent to a small town in Maine." He took the cooler onto the porch where three Muskoka chairs made of red cedar looked out over the dark lake. Jim sank into one and handed Leon and me another beer when we joined him.

I told him about Paris, and the fact that I'd let a *satori* slip through the Society's fingers. I told him about my trip to the British Museum and the ritual that had recovered my memories, aided by the statue of the god Hapi. And I

44

told him about the magic that had been awoken at the same time as my memories, seemingly powered by magical circles and symbols that were etched into my bones.

When I was finished, Jim asked, "What did your dad say when you confronted him about the magic powers?"

"I haven't confronted him yet. I was waiting to see if any more memories returned." I took a sip of the ice-cold beer. "But I remember everything now. He got the Coven to put an enchantment on me when I was just a kid."

"That's crazy, man," Jim said, looking out over the dark lake and shaking his head slowly. "What kind of father would do that to his son?"

"You know what my dad's like. The Society of Shadows is the most important thing in his life. It comes before his own family."

Jim nodded. "Yeah, I know." He looked over at Leon. "And what about you, my friend? What's your story?"

Leon shrugged. "It's kinda boring compared to you guys. I'm just an app developer and computer programmer. My story isn't exciting."

"Don't let him fool you," I told Jim. "He's a good fighter and he's helped me out on more than one occasion."

"I get bored easily," Leon said. "Fighting bad guys is the only thing that breaks the monotony."

"So you like excitement?" Jim asked. "Well, you should get plenty of that tomorrow if we find the nightwing's lair. Those things don't die easily."

"Have you ever killed one before?" Leon asked.

Jim shook his head. "No. Nightwings are rare and usually keep to themselves. There's plenty of lore about them, though, especially from a few centuries ago when they were regarded as demons and even dragons in Europe. Maybe they got tired of being hunted and that's why they went into hiding. How about you, Alec? You ever kill one?"

"No," I said. "I've never even seen one. Like you said, they're rare."

"It's a shame we have to kill it," Jim said, looking out over the lake again, reflectively.

I knew what he meant. If the lore was correct, nightwings had been hunted extensively hundreds of years ago in Europe as demons and were now an endangered species, even though that status wasn't official because they didn't officially exist.

If it weren't for the fact that it was killing people, I'd leave the creature alone. But I'd seen the remains of Michael Roland torn open in a tent and Jeanette Gautier's eviscerated body discarded in a tree. I couldn't let the nightwing live, knowing that it would kill more people. If I did nothing, the creature's future victims' blood would be on my hands.

"We don't have a choice," I said.

Jim nodded. "Yeah, I know."

I finished my beer and put the empty bottle on the deck next to my chair as my phone began buzzing in my pocket. The signal wasn't strong around Jim's house but it was better than in the park. I checked the screen. It was Felicity. "Felicity, are you still awake?" I asked as I answered the call. "I didn't expect you to call me until the morning."

"It's fine," she said. "I couldn't sleep anyway. I did some research. There are no recorded cases of a nightwing marking its territory like that. It's unheard of. Nightwings don't do that sort of thing. They spend most of their time trying to stay hidden, not attracting attention to themselves."

"I'm going to put you on speaker," I said. "Jim Walker and Leon are here." I hit the speaker button and placed the phone on the arm of my chair.

"Hello, everyone," Felicity said. After Jim and Leon had replied, she told them what she'd told me.

"We think we found where its lair might be," I told her. "We're going there in the morning."

"If you bring back any information about the creature, it would be a great help for other investigators in the future," she said. "I can apply to have it uploaded to the Society's database."

"We can get some photos of the lair and the creature," Jim said. "I'll put it all in my report."

"Excellent." Felicity added, "Please be careful, all of you. This nightwing is acting unpredictably, so you need be on your guard."

"We will," I said. "And we're going to get plenty of rest tonight so we can go hunting early in the morning."

"All right," she said. "Goodnight."

"Goodnight, Felicity." I ended the call and put the phone in my pocket. I would have liked to speak with her some more but she was right, we needed to get to bed if we were going to be in fighting mode tomorrow. And it sounded like she hadn't gotten any sleep herself. I'd call her tomorrow when we'd dealt with the nightwing and have more of a conversation with her then.

"I guess we should get some sleep," I said to Leon and Jim.

"Sounds like a good idea," Leon said. "Traveling all day is tiring."

"I'll show you your room." Jim got out of his chair and drained his beer bottle. "Alec, you might as well have your old room."

"Sure," I said. "See you guys in the morning." I grabbed my suitcase and went into the house, through the kitchen, and along the corridor that led to "my" room.

Although I'd never actually lived with Jim—when I'd worked as his assistant, I'd lived in a Society-appointed apartment in Huntsville—there had been many evenings when Jim and I had spent long hours discussing cases and I'd stayed over. Eventually, the room at the end of the corridor became known as my room.

I opened the door and entered the room. It felt immediately familiar and welcoming to me even though I hadn't been here in a while.

There was a small bookshelf by the window and on its shelves were the books I'd been reading when I'd stayed here: a book on magical orders throughout history and a couple of grimoires that detailed summoning and banishing spells. On the shelf above these was a collection of paperback novels I'd read in here or out on the deck during summers past.

I wondered if I'd been happier back then, a rookie investigator getting involved with his first cases, excited at using magic to fight evil, learning new things from Jim. Looking back, those days sure felt happier.

Sitting on the bed, I looked out of the window at the dark lake. A lot had happened since those early days of being an investigator. I'd learned about the magical inscriptions on my bones, discovered the location of the Spear of Destiny—an artifact highly sought after by the forces of evil—and I'd found out that my mother's death hadn't been the accident everyone thought it had been.

The Society of Shadows, which had once seemed like a shining beacon of all that was good in the world, the last bastion against the forces of the supernatural, was now fighting inner corruption, compromised by its eternal enemy, the Midnight Cabal.

Nothing was like it used to be.

I told myself to snap out of it. Hell, I'd been traveling all day so I was probably just tired. I probably just needed to get some rest.

Undressing quickly, I slipped into the familiar bed and closed my eyes, falling asleep as if I were sliding down a long, muddy tunnel into darkness.

* * *

That night, I dreamed of Mallory. I was standing in a misty forest and I could see lights through the trees. I moved in that direction but I couldn't feel the ground beneath my feet. Looking down, I saw only the mist. I was still able to pass between the trees toward the lights by simply willing myself to move in that direction.

I reached a clearing where a Victorian house rose out of the mist, its windows seeming like eyes regarding me as I stood before it. All the lights inside were burning and I could hear dance music emanating from inside, the bass thudding like a heartbeat.

I drifted up the steps and onto the porch. The music was louder now, the beat of the bass vibrating through the house, myself, and the surrounding woods. Two polished brass numbers on the door declared the house to be number 19 and I wondered why a house in the middle of nowhere would need a number at all.

I could hear laughter and whoops of excitement beneath the constantly thrumming music. It sounded like there was a party happening inside.

I reached for the brass doorknob and the instant I touched it, the music stopped. The lights in the house went out, plunging the clearing into total darkness. The laughter and voices inside the house died.

The door swung open, revealing a dark foyer beyond, lit by moonlight creeping in through the windows. There were bodies lying on the floor and the smell of death drifted in the air.

I was about to turn away and leave the house when I heard Mallory's voice inside. "Alec, I'm here."

I stepped inside instantly. "Mallory?"

"Alec." Her voice came from upstairs. I looked up the wide, moonlit staircase that led from the foyer to the level above, flanked by ornate balustrades topped with carved gargoyle heads. There were more dead bodies on the stairs. I glanced down as I stepped over them—my ability to drift gone—and realized they were all in their late teens.

"Mallory?" I called again. "Where are you?"

I reached the top of the stairs and suddenly felt a cold, malevolent presence behind me. I whirled around. All I could see was a passageway leading into darkness but I still felt as if I was being watched by cold, unfeeling eyes.

"Alec." The voice was faint but it was unmistakably Mallory's. I walked along the passageway, straining my ears to hear any sound that would tell me where she was or give away the location of the malevolent presence I felt in the house. I passed closed doors on both sides, pausing to listen at each one.

I didn't dare open any of them. A cold finger of fear had settled on the back of my neck. I wouldn't open any door until I was sure Mallory was behind it.

"Mallory," I called, "speak to me." As soon as the words left my mouth, I wished I could take them back. They sounded too loud in the deserted passageway. The thing in the house was sure to hear me.

"I'm here," Mallory said, and I was sure the words came from the door in front of me.

I opened it and entered a small, dusty room with bare boards on the floor and no furnishings except for a full-length mirror in the center of the room.

"Alec." The voice came from the mirror.

I rubbed dust off the glass with my sleeve and gazed into it. Mallory's face looked back at me, her dark eyes frightened. She recognized me and pressed her hands against the glass from her side. "Alec, you found me."

"Where are you?" I asked. All I could see behind her was darkness.

"I don't know," she said, "but I'm glad you're here too."

I frowned. "I'm not there with you. I'm on the other side of this mirror. I'm dreaming."

She looked worried. "No, you can't be dreaming. This has to be real. It has to be real because if it's a dream, I can't wake up."

The image in the mirror began to shimmer and shift until Mallory was gone and in her place was a darker-skinned woman wearing a white *kalasiris*, the simple sheath dress worn by women in ancient Egypt. The dress was adorned with beads and feathers.

The woman's hair was black as midnight, worn long with the bangs held back by a simple gold headpiece. Her face was angular and pretty, her eyes outlined with kohl.

I stepped back from the mirror, surprised by the sudden transformation. What the hell had just happened? Where was Mallory?

As quickly as the woman had appeared, she disappeared and in her place stood Mallory again.

"Mallory, who was that?"

"You saw her?" she asked, her voice sounding hopeful.

I nodded. "Yeah, I saw her."

"It's Tia. The sorceress. She's been with me ever since I stabbed her heart and cursed myself. She's…inside me somehow."

"What do you mean? What does she want?"

"Revenge. She wants to destroy Rekhmire. She's helping me too, helping me track down Mr. Scary." She looked at the blackness around her, at something I couldn't see beyond the edge of the mirror. "That's how I got here." Looking back at me, she said, "Alec, are you still there?"

The image in the mirror began to dim, Mallory fading away and the glass merely reflecting the empty room behind me like any normal mirror.

"Mallory!"

"Alec, I can't hear you anymore. Are you still there?"

Then she was gone. I stood back from the mirror and felt that other, malevolent, presence in the house again. Whatever it was, it was searching for me, reaching out with its senses, hunting its prey with a cold, deadly determination.

I fled back down the moonlit staircase, avoiding the bodies littered over the steps, and ran for the door. It stood open, the dark woods beyond offering a place to hide from whatever was hunting me.

A moment before I reached the threshold, I felt an icy darkness inside the house reach for me, trying to grab me and pull me back, but I leaped forward, out of the house and onto the porch. I stumbled and rolled, regaining my feet quickly and turning back to the door to face whatever was coming out of it to get me.

But the door was closed. The lights were burning inside the house again and the steady thrum of dance music vibrated through the walls and out into the clearing.

I was floating above the ground again, my feet shrouded in mist.

When I woke up, I was bathed in sweat, confused and disorientated. Everything around me seemed unfamiliar for a moment, then slowly came into focus. I was in Jim's house, in my old room.

I'd had either a nightmare or a vision, or a combination of both.

Whether it had been just a dream or something more, one thing was for sure: I had to contact Mallory and make sure she was okay.

I picked up my phone from the nightstand and called her number. As usual, I got her voicemail. "Mallory, it's me again. I'm really worried about you so can you please call or text me as soon as you get this? Thanks." I hung up, wondering if someone at the Society could put a trace on Mallory's phone and tell me where it was. If I kept getting no reply, I was going to have to look into that option.

I respected Mallory's need for privacy but now I was afraid she wasn't answering her phone because she was unable to for some reason. I knew her and knew that even if she didn't want to speak to me, she'd send a text saying she was okay and telling me to stop bugging her.

Putting the phone back on the nightstand, I settled down into the bed again, staring up at the ceiling. I doubted I'd get much sleep after the nightmare but soon my eyelids felt heavy and the room around me faded away.

If I dreamed again that night, I didn't remember it.

CHAPTER 6

THE NEXT MORNING, WE BUMPED along a narrow, rocky trail in Jim's Jeep. Leon was in the passenger seat and I was in the back with the weapons and magical items we'd brought along.

We'd left the highway behind a couple of hours ago and Jim had navigated the Jeep alongside roads and trails, sometimes going off-road for a while before picking up another trail. Soon, this trail would end and we'd have to hike the rest of the way to the nightwing's lair.

"It went a long way to get to those people it killed," Leon said.

"The distance isn't all that far for a winged creature," Jim said. "Some sea birds can fly thousands of miles before needing to land. The nightwing would have no problem reaching its victims."

"The weird thing," I said, "is that it's decided to do so in the first place."

"This is as far as we go in the Jeep," Jim said, skidding to a stop and killing the engine. He opened his door, got out, and came around the back. I passed him the backpacks and weapons before sliding out into the morning sunshine.

We'd packed the equipment this morning, standing around Jim's kitchen table. Each of us had an enchanted sword and dagger. Jim had a full-size crossbow and I had a pistol crossbow. Leon had a shotgun with shells containing silver, the shells I usually called "Werewolf Stunners." We had no reason to believe the nightwing was affected by silver but we had no reason to disbelieve it either.

We each had a faerie stone in our pocket as well as a Maglite and a compass. The backpacks contained mundane gear such as waterproof clothing, food, climbing rope, harnesses, carabiners, first-aid kits, and water. Hunting a nightwing was dangerous enough but wandering into a dense forest held its own risks. Jim's pack also held a Nikon DSLR camera so he could document the creature and its lair for Felicity.

We had our phones with us but there was zero signal out here in the backcountry.

"Everyone ready?" Jim asked after Leon and I had strapped the swords and daggers to our belts and hefted the backpacks over our shoulders. We nodded, and he said, "Let's go," taking off at a rapid pace through the trees.

Leon and I followed, avoiding low-hanging branches and stepping over rocks and fallen trees while we tried to keep pace with Jim. I tried to remember how old Jim was and then realized I'd never known his age. Whatever his age, and despite his muscular bulk, he could outpace someone much younger, as he was doing now. We were almost jogging just to keep up with his long, rapid stride.

"This isn't a race, man," Leon said after a few minutes.

Jim looked over his shoulder, realized we were lagging behind, and slowed down. "Sorry, I usually walk these woods alone. I forgot how difficult this terrain is to move through if you're not used to it."

He checked the map while he waited for us to catch up. "In four miles, we should come to the top of a ridge ahead. Beyond that is the area we marked on the map, the place where we should find the beast."

It took us almost two hours to reach the top of the ridge. By the time we got there, I'd seen enough fir trees to last me a lifetime. Leon sat on the ground and opened his pack, taking out a bottle of water. I did the same, wishing I'd put the water in a cooler when the warm liquid entered my mouth.

Jim had scouted ahead to the edge of the ridge and was looking over it, hands on hips, hair blowing in the slight breeze, looking like he should be modeling clothes in a menswear catalog.

He looked back at Leon and me and pointed down over the edge of the ridge. "Down there."

We stowed our water and joined him. There was a valley ahead of us, its floor rocky and littered with fallen trees. A stream ran among the rocks before disappearing beneath the trees. The walls of the valley were rock and I could see fissures and caves near ground level and higher up toward the top of the ridge on the other side. I assumed there were similar caves and faults in the rock wall we stood atop but they were impossible to see from where we were.

This was perfect nightwing country.

"How do we get down there?" Leon asked.

I looked along the ridge. There was no easy way down. So, dropping my pack and taking out a coil of climbing rope, I said, "We climb down."

Leon stepped away from the edge, holding his hands up in protest. "Whoa, wait a minute. You didn't say anything about rock climbing."

"We won't be climbing," I said, "we'll be rappelling. Don't worry, you'll be perfectly safe as long as you do exactly what Jim and I tell you." I found the carabiners in my pack and laid them out on the ground, as well as the metal figure-8 devices that would be used to create enough friction when feeding the rope through them to rappel at a steady pace.

"I don't know about this," Leon said. "It's a long way down." He looked over the edge and swallowed.

Jim was taking the nylon harnesses from his pack. "Leon, do you trust Alec?"

Leon nodded without hesitation. "Yes."

"Then you should know that he's done this many times before and he won't let anything happen to you."

Leon looked at me, his eyes worried.

"I know it's scary," I told him, "but I'll look after you every step of the way, okay?"

He nodded slowly. "Okay."

I took a harness from Jim and showed it to Leon. "You'll be wearing this. It's made of nylon and it's strong. This figure-eight device fixes to the front of the harness like this." I attached it using a carabiner. "The rope goes through this hole here and you can let yourself down as slowly as you want just by feeding the rope through your hands. We're going to put the rope around the trunk of that big pine tree over there. It's going to be okay."

Leon nodded. His hands were shaking. "I believe you."

"I'll go first," I said, "to show you how it's done. Then you come down after me and then Jim will come down last, okay?"

"Sure."

I attached a figure-8 to my own harness. Jim ran the rope around the big pine tree I'd indicated earlier and handed both strands to me. I pushed them through the hole in the figure-8 and leaned back, putting all my weight on the rope to test it. It was firm.

I showed Leon how to control the rate of descent using his hands, then stepped backward over the edge of the ridge. I rappelled to the rocks below and gave Jim a thumbs-up. He pulled the rope back up and prepared Leon for his descent.

There was a smell of decay in the air where I stood. It smelled as if some fish had died, their carcasses rotting on the rocks in the sun. I looked around for the source but couldn't see any dead fish anywhere.

The rope was thrown over the ridge again and Leon appeared at the top, leaning backward and looking over his shoulder at me.

"Don't look down," I told him. "You're doing great. Now just walk backward. Keep the soles of your boots on the rock wall and your legs straight."

He was doing fine. He descended a few feet and I could sense him gaining his confidence. He'd stopped shaking, at least.

The fish smell hit me again and I looked over at the stream, my eyes following its course to where it ran into the woods. I thought I saw movement there, in the shadows beneath the trees, but it was only fleeting and was probably a trick of the light.

I raised a hand to shield my eyes against the morning sun but it didn't help any. I felt a prickle on the back of my neck but reminded myself that it could be a deer in there, or a raccoon.

Turning my attention back to Leon, I said, "Not far now." He was about fifty feet from the ground, descending slowly but seeming to have conquered his fear. Once his boots touched the ground, he'd probably feel great and want to do it again.

I heard a sound coming from the woods. There was something big in there, splashing through the water and crashing through the branches. I turned in that direction just in time to see a huge bulk burst from the trees and take to the air.

I drew my sword before I'd even registered the details of the creature's appearance, but as it glided down the valley toward me, I could see a huge snout, large yellow eyes and wide ears like a bat's.

Its body was long and sinuous and was covered in dark brown fur that was black in places. The wingspan was at least thirty feet, the wings themselves black and membranous, stretched over long bones that protruded from the creature's back.

It had two densely-muscled forearms and clawed hands. Its scaly hind feet were equipped with deadly-looking talons.

I could see how these creatures had been mistaken for dragons in past times, especially since they were only seen at night, in moonlight. I had no idea why this one was awake during the daylight and I didn't have time to think about that now; the beast was gliding toward Leon, who was hanging fifty feet in the air like a snack on a rope.

I sheathed the sword and prepared the pistol crossbow. "Jim," I called, "we have trouble."

"I see it."

I looked up to where he stood atop the ridge, loading his crossbow.

The nightwing—although I wasn't sure I could call it that now since it was hunting in the day—curled back its lips, revealing a set of wickedly-sharp teeth designed to rip through flesh.

"Leon, use the shotgun," I urged.

Leon nodded grimly and fumbled with the gun, trying to get it off his shoulder while in his precarious position.

I fired at the creature, aiming for its eye. Maybe if I could cause it enough pain, it would retreat, or at least forget about Leon for a moment. My bolt lodged in the beast's snout, seeming to cause about as much pain as a pinprick.

It continued on its course, yellow eyes fixed on Leon.

Jim fired his crossbow. I hoped the full-sized bolt might do more damage than my smaller one. It hit the nightwing's head but, instead of penetrating the skin, it skimmed across it and fell to the rocks below with a clatter.

Leon had the shotgun in his hands now and he was taking aim, steadying himself against the rock wall with his boots, keeping his legs straight and still.

The creature was swooping along the wall now, its body parallel with the vertical rock face.

Leon shot at it and I wished we'd brought a rifle instead of the shotgun. The shot scattered uselessly and the creature kept on coming.

I threw the pistol crossbow to the ground and ran for the rope, grabbing it with both hands and positioning my boots against the rock. I began to climb. There was no way I could beat the creature to Leon but I wanted to be as close as I could get because my next move must not fail. There was no room for error.

I got about ten feet from the ground before time ran out. The nightwing would reach Leon in seconds. He'd drawn his sword, the blade glowing bright blue in his hand, and was preparing to fight for his life.

I hoped it wouldn't come to that. I summoned my rage, feeling it glowing inside me like a white heat. With one hand on the rope to support myself, I raised the other in the direction of the creature. Blue energy crackled around my palm, forming magical symbols in the air. I let the power go, thrusting my hand forward as I did so. The magical energy shot from my palm toward the creature, striking its chest.

The nightwing slammed into the rock wall, a roar of pain escaping its throat. It began to fall to the ground, spreading its wings in an attempt to gain air again.

I resumed my climb, checking the creature's whereabouts as I attempted to reach Leon. It had regained its composure and was flapping its wings, wheeling its body so that it flew back the way it had come. I had a feeling it was only retreating so it could come swooping back this way for another attack.

"Leon, come down to me," I said.

He dropped down another twenty or so feet and I climbed higher up the rope to meet him. The nightwing had gained altitude after its fall and was angling around to face us.

I began to summon a magical shield that would protect both of us. As I felt the energy building up inside me, something different happened. In my mind's eye, I saw a magic circle, burning brightly as if it were made of green fire. A complex pattern of pentagrams, hexagrams, and Enochian letters filled the circle, glowing like fiery jade.

I concentrated on the pattern and felt the energy of my magical shield grow.

The nightwing was gliding along the rock wall toward us now, increasing its speed with powerful flicks of its membranous wings. I extended the shield around us and concentrated on the magic circle in my mind to strengthen it. I was going to pay a hell of a price for this later but, right now, I had to protect Leon and myself from the creature swooping toward us.

Jim loosed another crossbow bolt and managed to embed this one into the nightwing's back. The creature bellowed but still came for us, fury burning in its yellow eyes.

I pushed everything I had into the shield. The nightwing hit it head on. A sickening crunch filled the air as something broke in the creature, probably its neck. It plummeted to the ground like a dead weight, crashing onto the rocks below.

"Come on," I told Leon, climbing down the rope as quickly as I dared. I wasn't attached to anything, relying on the strength in my arms and legs to keep me from falling. If that strength suddenly failed, as it always did after I fed my energy into shields and magical blasts, I'd drop to the rocks and at least break a few bones if not crack my skull open.

Leon followed me down and when we got to the bottom, I went over to check the nightwing. It was dead. If hitting the magical shield at full force hadn't killed it, then the fall had.

I detached Leon from the rope and told him to wait for Jim to come down. I already felt weak and I needed to find a place to rest. These rocks wouldn't cut it.

"You okay, man?" Leon asked, putting a hand on my shoulder.

"I'll be okay in a little while," I said, heading for the stream. There was a grassy back on the other side beneath some trees that would be a better place to lie on the ground than here.

The stream was only a couple of feet deep so I waded through the water to the other side. When I reached the grass, I sat down and waited for my strength to drain away as it had every other time I'd used magic.

I closed my eyes and another magic circle appeared in my mind. This one was bright red, with a unicursal hexagram inside along with Egyptian hieroglyphs. I had no idea what it was supposed to do but I concentrated on it. It had appeared at this moment, so it must serve some function. I was starting to trust the magic within me, the power that had been magically grafted to my bones.

As soon as I concentrated on the red magical symbol, the energy drain halted. My strength didn't sap away until I was lying helpless on the ground. Instead, I felt exactly the same as I had before the drain had started.

I opened my eyes, the burning red circle still visible in my mind, overlaying the valley around me, but fading. Once it had disappeared completely, I knew I was going to retain all my energy.

"So there's a failsafe," I said to myself. "Why the hell didn't I know about this before?" I stood up and leaned against a red pine, taking a deep breath and making sure beyond all doubt that I wasn't going to collapse. I felt fine.

Then something dropped out of the tree and landed at my feet. I looked down. It was a crow. A dead crow.

There was another rustling and a gray jay fell from a nearby tree, followed by a couple of chickadees. Then a squirrel hit the ground a few feet away. Like the birds, it was dead.

I heard noises from the stream and looked over there in time to see a swarm of midges suddenly drop into the water. The surface of the stream was broken by the bodies of a dozen dead fish rising to the surface and floating there, bellies up.

Jim had rappelled all the way down and was sorting out the rope. Leon was walking over to me.

"Leon, get back!" I shouted at him.

He stopped, confused, standing on the opposite bank of the stream and frowning at me. "What is it, Alec?"

"Don't come near me. Not right now. Something's happening." I looked at the dead animals and fish around me, feeling bad because I must have caused it. It would have been better if I'd let my energy become depleted and then slowly recovered.

What if I'd been standing near Leon and concentrating on the red magical symbol? Would my friend be lying dead on the ground instead of these animals?

I felt that the danger had passed, that these animals had been drained of life while the red Egyptian symbols had been glowing in my mind and that as soon as the magic circle had faded, the death spell, or whatever, was done.

But I couldn't risk Leon's life to find out if I was safe to be around.

I noticed a chipmunk regarding me from a nearby rock. He was holding a seed in his paws but his attention was on me, his black eyes staring into mine.

I crouched down and held out my hand as if I had a tasty treat for him. The chipmunk approached me warily, moving in short bursts, stopping between each one to check me out. When he got close enough to my hand to sniff it and discover I had no food after all, he scampered away behind the rock. He was pissed at me but he was still alive.

Turning to Leon, I said, "I think it's okay now." I waded back across the stream to where he stood.

"What's wrong?" he asked.

"I'll tell you later when I figure it out myself. Right now, we need to get some photos of that nightwing and find its lair."

Jim was already snapping away with the Nikon when we got over to the body. "I can't figure out why it's out here in the day," he said. "See those large eyes and ears? They're adapted for night hunting."

"Let's find its lair," I said. "Maybe there'll be something there that explains it."

"What about the body?" Leon asked. "Aren't we going to bury it or something?"

"The local wildlife will take care of it," I said. If this area were less remote, burying the body would be a good idea. But out here in the middle of nowhere, it wasn't necessary. Animals and birds would eat the nightwing's flesh and the bones would eventually be scattered.

We followed the stream toward the trees, looking for the creature's lair.

"Over there," Leon said, pointing at a cave in the rock wall we'd rappelled down. There were plenty of caves in the valley but what set this one apart was a jumble of bones and skulls outside its entrance.

Jim drew his sword and Leon and I followed suit. Bathed in the blue glow from the blades, we picked our way over the rocks to the cave entrance.

The fissure was shaped like an inverted V and went deeper into the rocks than the glow from our blades could penetrate. The dead fish smell was stronger here, emanating from a pile of discarded carcasses on the ground.

Jim bent down and inspected some of the skulls. "You ever see anything like this?" he asked me, holding up a skull that had a dog-like shape but with a ridge of sharp bone running from between the eye sockets to the back of the cranium.

"No.".

"How about this?" He held up a second skull that looked human except for two horns.

"Demon, maybe," I suggested.

Jim nodded, sifting through the bones. "Apart from the fish, these all look demon." He stood up and looked around the valley. "Where the hell did they come from?"

"I think the answer is in your question," I told him.

He shot me a look. "Okay, smartass, let me rephrase that. How the hell did they get here?"

"No idea," I said, "but you might want to get some pictures for Felicity."

He used the Nikon to document the scene.

"If that nightwing has been eating demons," I said, "that could explain why it went crazy. Demon bodies are full of all kinds of poisons."

Jim thought about that and nodded. "Yeah, that makes sense. The poison could have affected its mind and made it attack humans."

I looked into the blackness of the cave. Maybe there were answers in the creature's lair. "I'm going to take a look in there."

"I'll keep watch out here," Jim said. "If there are demons in the area, we need to be cautious."

"Good idea," I said. "You coming, Leon?"

Leon nodded. Jim handed him the Nikon, which Leon slung over his shoulder.

We entered the cave, guided by the blue glow from our swords. The passageway looked barely wide enough for the nightwing to pass through but there was evidence that the creature had been here; its claws had left scratches on the rocks and there was a strong smell of death in the air. This was definitely a hunter's lair.

The passageway opened up into a circular space where a bed of pine branches lay on the floor. A half-eaten corpse had been shoved up against the wall, as if the nightwing were saving it for later.

I went over to the body and held my sword over it, examining it in the blue light.

Most of the face, neck, and chest had been eaten and from the condition of the ragged, dark red flesh, I guessed that the demon had been dead less than twenty-four hours.

It was naked and I could see a tattoo on its left wrist. "Leon, get a shot of this," I said. Demons sometimes wore tattoos that showed their allegiance to a certain master or displayed the symbol of their clan.

The tattoo on this one's arm was of a double-headed ax inside a triangle. I didn't recognize it but a little research should tell us more about this demon and where it came from.

Leon took a couple of photos and we left the cave.

When we got outside, Jim was standing by the woods. He waved us over.

"I think that's how the demons got here," he said, pointing into the trees.

There was a small clearing on the other side of the stream and in the clearing stood a stone circle. The stones had been carved with a knotwork design that seemed to represent a cross within a circle.

"A portal," I said.

"Yeah." Jim took the camera from Leon and got some pictures. "But what's it doing here and where does it lead?"

We waded across the stream to the stones. They were huge but buried deep in the earth so that the part of them that was above ground stood waist-high. The larger stones were arranged around a smaller, inner circle of knee-high stones carved with the same knotwork pattern.

"This symbol isn't demonic," I said, tracing my fingers over the design. "It's faerie."

Jim frowned. "Why would demons be using a faerie circle? None of this makes sense."

"Hey, guys, something's happening," Leon said, pointing to a half dozen sparkles of light that had begun drifting up from the ground.

The stone I was touching suddenly grew warm.

"It's being activated," I said. "We need to get out of the circle."

We backed off as the sparkles of light increased in number. They floated up from the ground within the circle, twisting and interweaving until they became a light so bright it was difficult to look at.

We hid behind nearby trees, sheathing our swords so the glow wouldn't give us away. The light from the circle filled the woods for an instant and then died just as quickly.

I peered around the trunk of my tree to see a woman standing in the center of the circle. She had long blond hair that was decorated with brightly-colored flowers and wore a long white dress over a bountiful figure.

She looked around for a moment before calling out, "Alec, I know you're there. It's time for you to repay your debt to me."

CHAPTER 7

CRAP," I SAID WHEN I realized who the woman was. The Lady of the Forest, the faerie queen that Leon and I had encountered when we'd traveled to Faerie in search of James Robinson, the victim of a changeling. I'd struck a bargain with the Lady in exchange for passage out of Faerie, but the terms had been that her envoy would offer me various ways to repay my debt and I was free to refuse each time, although I'd be in the Lady's debt until I accepted one of the offers. The terms said nothing about her appearing in a stone circle and demanding repayment.

I stepped out from behind the tree and walked to the circle. Leon and Jim followed.

"What the hell do you want?" I asked her.

"Alec," she said, "you're a hard man to find." She smiled and I felt like my insides were melting. She may

74

have pissed me off by turning up like this but she was a faerie and that meant her beauty exceeded that of human women. There was also a glamour spell around her, as evidenced by a tattoo on my left shoulder growing hotter.

"If I'm so hard to find, how come you found me here, in the middle of nowhere, in Canada?"

She pouted, pursing her luscious lips. "You don't sound pleased to see me."

"There's a reason for that," I said.

She sighed with frustration. "Perhaps you might be friendlier toward me if I looked more human." The air around her shimmered and her form became blurry. When she came back into focus, she was still stunning, only now it was as if the Beauty Meter had been turned down from 11 out of 10 to an 8 or 9. She wore boots, jeans, and a green-check shirt. Her hair was loosely curled in an eighties-style perm. The blooming flowers were all gone, except for the white lily that represented my debt to her.

"Do you like it?" she asked, spinning around slowly.

I sighed. "Please, just tell me what you want."

Pointing to the white lily in her hair, she said, "I want you to repay your debt."

"No, we made a deal that your envoy would visit me and offer me various tasks and I would be able to refuse them. You turning up here like this wasn't part of our agreement."

She folded her arms and pouted again. "Well, things have changed. This was the only was I could reach you."

"Our agreement hasn't changed. We made a fair exchange—an exchange that is binding according to the laws of interaction between faeries and humans. You can't just change that. I can refuse your request and there's nothing you can do about it."

She stepped out of the stone circle and came toward us. "Please, Alec, I don't have anywhere else to turn. You're my only hope." She put on a worried expression and even wrung her hands in a performance that might have won her an Academy Award during the days of silent movie melodrama, but I knew she was only trying to play me.

"You're overplaying the emotion," I told her. "And your plea doesn't really make sense, because the last time I saw you, you were sitting on a throne, being served by faerie warriors and human slaves."

She looked wistful for a moment and then sadness darkened her face. "As I said, things have changed."

"Alec," Jim whispered, "she may be able to help us. She came through the portal so she knows what's on the other side. Maybe she also knows how these demons got here and why they're using a faerie circle."

"She's a faerie," I told him. "You know how dangerous they are. We can't trust her."

"But if you're already in debt to her anyway, maybe you should listen to what she has to say. We help her and she helps us."

"Accepting her help is why I'm in debt in the first place. I don't want to get you and Leon involved in that."

"Okay," Jim said, "but all I'm saying is we need help. We came here to kill the nightwing, which we did, but it turns out the nightwing was stopping something even worse from coming through that portal. Your friend here…"

"She isn't my friend."

"It's just a figure of speech, Alec, don't take it so personally. This faerie might have information we need to close this case. We can't just walk away now, knowing that a horde of demons could come through that portal at any second. At least ask her what's on the other side."

The Lady of the Forest looked at me with imploring eyes.

I could see Jim's point, but dealing with her put a bad taste in my mouth. "Before you tell me what you want from me, I want something from you. If you give me some information I can use, then I might consider helping you. Do you know anything about the demons using this stone circle?"

"Demons?" She wrinkled her nose as if the hell-spawn were directly beneath it and she could smell their brimstone odor.

"She doesn't know anything," I said to Jim.

"Wait, I didn't say that," she said quickly. "Tell me more about these demons."

"If you know about them, you tell me," I said.

She hesitated, her brow furrowing.

"I'm waiting," I said.

She held up a hand. "I'm thinking."

"She doesn't know anything," I repeated to Jim.

"Maybe not," he admitted.

"Sorry," I said to the Lady, "you don't have any information that can help me so I don't have time to pay off my debt to you right now because I'm busy working a case. So I refuse your…"

"Wait!" she said. "The ax."

I waited for more information. When none came, I prompted her. "The ax?"

"On their bodies. The symbol of the ax. Those are the demons you mean?"

"All right," I said. "Tell me more. Where do they come from? Why are they using a faerie ring to travel here?"

She smiled, a flash of wickedness in her icy blue eyes. She waggled a finger at me as if scolding a naughty child. "Not so fast, Alec. I've proven to you that I have information you need. I can't just give it away, especially to someone who is already in my debt."

"I'm not making any more deals with you," I said.

She put on a pained expression. "You make it sound so bad, as if dealing with me were the wickedest thing in the world. I'm not one of those demons, you know, I'm a faerie. A being of light. Of beauty. Of passion."

Her words slid into my mind and invaded my thoughts. The protection tattoo on my left shoulder began to heat up in warning.

"Get out of my head," I told her.

She sighed. "You're no fun. All right, I won't ask for an exchange. I will simply announce my terms as follows: if you agree to assist me, your debt will be fulfilled and I will also tell you everything I know about the demons. Do we have a deal?"

"Not until I know exactly how you want me to assist you."

"What? I'm giving you the demon information for free and you still think I'm trying to trick you?"

I shrugged. Bargains with faeries were notoriously tricky, in some cases even deadly, so I wasn't taking any chances.

The Lady threw up her arms in frustration. "Very well. All I ask is your protection for three days and three nights. Simple. Do this and your debt to me will be paid. There, now the terms are stated clearly. Do you agree to them?"

"Hold on. Protect you from what? Where are all your faerie guards? Why aren't they protecting you?"

"They're dead. So, let's make this exchange now, and in three days, it will be over. You will be able to go on with your life, your debt to me paid in full."

"It's the 'going on with my life' part I'm worried about. Who's after you? You had a small army of faerie warriors to protect you and they're all dead? What makes you think I won't end up the same way?"

She looked into my eyes. "I believe you are a strong warrior. Since this lily flowered, I've been watching you, Alec. I keep track of all who owe me a service, but in you I saw great bravery and strength that the others did not possess. You stopped an army of the dead. You fought monsters that were the things of nightmares. And now, I believe you can protect me where my own faerie guard failed."

"Tell me what I'm expected to protect you from," I said.

"Two vampires. They want something that only I know the location of."

"And what is this thing?"

"That's simply a detail. It does not concern you or affect the exchange between us. Do you accept the terms?"

"Give me a minute," I said. Taking Jim and Leon to one side, I said, "What do you guys think? Should I just refuse her and tell her to be on her way?"

Jim looked at me closely. "I know you, Alec. You won't turn away anyone who needs your help, even a faerie. If anything happened to her, you would never forgive yourself."

"Yeah," Leon agreed. "Besides, it'll cancel your debt, man. How hard can it be to protect her from two vampires for a few days?"

"The vampires killed her personal guard," I reminded him. But who was I kidding? Jim was right; I wouldn't turn the Lady away and leave her to her fate. She wasn't an evil creature but she was running from two that were. Even if I wasn't indebted to her, my job meant I couldn't ignore the chance to take out two powerful vampires.

"We'll help you," Leon told me.

"No, this is my debt. I don't want either of you involved."

Leon shook his head. "Just like we know you well enough to know you wouldn't turn the faerie away, you should know us well enough to know we wouldn't let you do this alone. Right, Jim?"

"That's right," Jim agreed.

"Thanks, guys," I said. "I mean that." I turned to the Lady and said, "I agree to protect you for three days and nights in exchange for the cancelation of my debt."

She let out a sigh of relief. "Excellent." Looking back at the stone circle, she said, "We should leave this place."

"We can't leave, we're working a case," I reminded her. "And you apparently have some information you're going to share regarding the demons that came through the portal."

"Oh, yes. They were chasing me, trying to catch me for those disgusting vampires. I came here and they followed. The creature in the cave killed them. It didn't hurt me, of course, because I've been here many times before and the creature knows me."

"So it ate the demons because they were chasing you?" Jim asked.

She nodded. "Yes, it saved my life. If I'd been taken back to those vampires, I would have been tortured until I revealed the location of my item."

"Did you know the creature went crazy after eating those demons?"

She seemed genuinely upset. Her blue eyes filled with tears that pooled on her lower lids. "Yes, poor thing. It even tried to attack me the next time I came through the portal. I didn't dare come through again after that. I hoped the creature's madness would pass so I used my magic to watch it. I saw it hunt down those people. And then your friend here,"—she indicated Jim with her hand—"was investigating the case and I needed to reach you, Alec, so it was fortuitous that he called you and brought you here."

I raised an eyebrow. It sounded too coincidental to me. "Was it just fortuitous, or was there more to it than that?"

She turned her eyes downward, a guilty look spreading over her face. "I may have prompted him to call you by showing him certain dreams when he was investigating the case. Dreams of him calling you and both of you solving the case together."

Jim was furious. "What? You manipulated me?"

"No, not at all. I simply put the idea in your head. You took it from there and called Alec."

"If you needed to reach me so badly, why did you bring me here? Why didn't you just come to my office?" I asked her.

She scoffed. "In that quaint little town you call home? It's probably crawling with Cabal members. I couldn't show my face there."

"Cabal? You mean the Midnight Cabal?"

"Yes, the vampires are members of the Midnight Cabal." She cast a glance at the stone circle. "We really should leave here."

Jim was seething. I put a hand on his shoulder and said, "Don't let her get to you."

"I did have those dreams," he said. "I dreamed that you and I solved the case together. I guess that was why I called you. If I'd known it was only a faerie trying to bring you here, I'd never have done it. Goddamn it, Alec, she got into my head."

I looked at the faerie queen. "So why didn't you just give me the dreams?"

"I couldn't. The Cabal has closed down most of my portals to this world. This one is ancient and can't be closed so easily. It was the only one I could use and you were too far away from here for me to influence your dreams."

"But you had no problem getting into my head," Jim said, frustrated. "I was close enough to be toyed with."

"Hey, don't sweat it," I told him. "She brought us back together and that's a good thing, no matter the reason for the reunion."

He nodded. "Yeah, I guess you're right."

"You know I am. Now, I suggest we get the hell out of here before something nasty comes through that portal and makes our day even worse."

CHAPTER 8

WE GOT TO THE JEEP two hours later. On the journey back, the only conversation had been about my cases in Dearmont and Jim's latest exploits. Leon had told us about the world of apps and how he'd gotten his ideas for the ones that had made him rich. The Lady of the Forest had walked a few feet behind us, arms folded like a sulking child.

No one had spoken of our current situation. It was as if we'd made an unspoken agreement to let our emotions cool down before we discussed it again. I felt duped by the Lady and no doubt Jim did too. So we'd made the entire two-hour hike without acknowledging the faerie queen's presence at all.

Now that we were at the Jeep, she spoke up, arms still folded and face still sulky. "I don't like being ignored."

"And we don't like being played," I said, stowing my backpack and weapons in the back of the Jeep.

She sighed loudly. "I'm sorry about the dreams I gave your friend, all right? I didn't know what else to do, how else to reach you."

"Remind me to give you my cell number," I said, opening the rear door and getting in. "Actually, no, don't. After this fiasco is over, I don't want you getting in touch with me ever again."

She got in next to me. Her demeanor seemed to have changed and now she looked excited. She looked around the interior of the Jeep with wide, eager eyes.

"You haven't been in a car before, have you?" I asked her.

She shook her head. "No, I was carried around on my throne by slaves."

I wasn't sure how to answer that so I just said, "Well, this is similar but it involves less subjugation of human beings."

"My slaves were totally willing," she told me. "They dedicated their lives to me, shunning your world to live in Faerie and serve me as their queen."

"You sure you didn't make them dream about it first so they'd do what you wanted?"

She huffed. "Can we please drop that now? I said I was sorry."

"No, you didn't. You need to apologize to Jim." I felt like I was chiding a child, not talking to a powerful faerie queen.

Jim and Leon got in the car.

"Jim, I'm sorry," the Lady said unemotionally. She turned to me with a contented look on her face. "There, I said it."

Jim looked at me in the rearview mirror and rolled his eyes.

Trying not to laugh, I turned to the faerie. "Do you have a name? Something we can call you instead of Lady of the Forest? If there are other humans around, that's going to sound a little weird."

She thought for a moment. "You would not be able to pronounce my real name." Then her face lit up. "Perhaps I can choose a human name."

"Okay," I said, "go for it."

"Gloria," she said immediately.

"Gloria?"

She nodded enthusiastically. "Gloria."

Jim started the engine and made a U-turn so we were headed back toward the highway on the narrow trail. "Gloria it is," he said.

"Tell us about the vampires that are hunting you," I said as we bumped along the trail.

"Their names are Davos and Korax and they rule the House of Zabat. I believe it goes back a long way. Ancient Greece or something."

I held up a hand, stopping her. "Ancient Greece? How old are these vampires?"

"I don't know. They've been around forever. The House of Zabat has always been feuding with certain factions in the Faerie realm, so when the Midnight Cabal began taking over parts of Faerie, Davos and Korax were only too willing to help them."

"The Cabal is taking over parts of Faerie," I repeated. "Why?"

The Lady—Gloria—sighed. "Parts of Faerie intersect with this world. The Midnight Cabal is trying to control those parts for some upcoming war they want to start. A war against your Society of Shadows."

"A war? I know they're the sworn enemies of the Society but this is the first I've heard of a war." My father had told me that the Midnight Cabal had resurfaced but he hadn't mentioned anything about a war. Was it something else he was keeping from me or was the Society unaware of the impending danger? As soon as I got a signal on my phone, I needed to call him and warn him.

Gloria shrugged. "I don't concern myself with petty feuds between humans."

"Until it affects you," I said. "I'm guessing the Cabal tried to do a land-grab that included the part of Faerie you ruled."

Sadness washed over her face. "Those vampires and their demon minions took my forest. I barely managed to escape with my life. I've been on the run ever since." She touched my arm lightly. "Now I have a protector. Thank you, Alec."

The tattoo on my left shoulder began to heat up again. "Stop trying to glamor me," I told her. "And I'm only your protector for three days, as per our agreement. After that, my debt is paid in full."

"Yes, of course," she said softly. "I was only expressing my gratitude. Sometimes I lose control and my magic just spills out everywhere."

"Okay, ground rule number one," I said firmly. "Keep it in your pants. No trying to glamor me, Leon, or Jim. Or anybody else, for that matter. Got it?"

She crossed her arms and turned to face the window. "Fine."

Jim caught my eye in the rearview again and raised his eyebrows. I knew exactly what he was thinking; the next three days weren't going to be plain sailing. As well as protecting Gloria from the vampires that were hunting her, we were going to have to deal with her facsimile of a human personality, which seemed to be that of a spoiled brat.

When we reached the highway a couple of hours later, I switched on my phone and checked for a signal. There was barely anything yet, so I put the phone back in my pocket. I didn't want the connection to drop while I was trying to warn the Society of an impending attack.

Jim slowed the Jeep. "Looks like Frasier and Girard are here."

Up ahead was the parking area where we'd stopped yesterday. A dark green Chevy Tahoe was parked by the side of the road and the two cops were standing next to it, watching as a blue Honda Civic was being winched up onto a tow truck.

Jim pulled up alongside the Tahoe and got out. "Hey, guys, how's it going?"

Girard looked over at Jim and shook his head as if in disgust. He was still wearing shades, along with the same sports jacket and tie he'd had on yesterday. "Back off, Walker. The real police are doing their job. Unless you think the car's haunted or something." He gave Jim a wide grin.

Detective Frasier took Jim gently by the arm and led him back to the Jeep. "Ignore, Girard," she said, "he must have gotten out of the wrong side of the bed again. You find anything?"

"Yeah, we dealt with the creature," Jim said. "It won't be giving you any more problems."

"What was it? Do I even want to know?"

"Not unless you want nightmares for a while. I can show you on the map where we left the body if you want to take Girard out there and prove to him the thing is real."

She shrugged. "No, he'd only say you faked it somehow."

"Then all you need to know is that the problem is dealt with."

"Thanks, Jim. And thanks to your friends, too." She looked into the Jeep and gave us all a friendly wave. When she saw Gloria, she looked surprised, then hid it with a smile. "Oh, hi there."

Gloria pressed the button that opened her window. It buzzed all the way down. "Hi, I'm Gloria," she told Frasier. Then she looked over her shoulder and gave me a conspiratorial wink.

I rolled my eyes.

"Hi, Gloria. I'm Detective Claire Frasier." She came up to the window and shook Gloria's hand. "Do you work with Jim?"

Gloria looked momentarily confused, as if she wanted to say something but couldn't. She frowned and then said, "Alec and I have a deal."

Frasier looked in at me through the window, a confused look on her face.

I offered her a weak smile. "Gloria means I'm helping her out with something."

A look of understanding crossed Frasier's face. She looked back at Gloria. "Oh, you're a client. I see. Well, good luck with whatever your problem is."

"Vampires," Gloria said. "And demons."

Frasier looked shocked. "Wow, that's some problem. Don't worry, I'm sure these guys will sort it out for you." She looked closer at Gloria. "Are you from around here?"

"No," Gloria said. "I'm from a place far away."

"Oh?" Frasier asked, waiting for Gloria to elaborate.

91

"We have to go," I said, reaching across Gloria and putting the window up. "Nice seeing you again."

"Okay," Frasier said, giving us another little wave. "Have a nice day."

When the window was all the way up and Jim had taken Claire away from the Jeep to talk further with her, I looked sharply at Gloria. "What the hell was that? 'Alec and I have a deal'?"

She shrugged. "I'm a faerie, I can't lie."

"But you're supposed to be good at deceiving people. What about all the humans you've dealt with in the past, using your faerie cunning to trick them? I didn't see any of that. Where was the faerie cunning?"

She looked flustered. "I don't know. She just threw me, all right? Having a conversation when there's a deal to be struck is one thing but just talking for the sake of it is something new to me."

"Well, don't get too used to it. My deal with you is three days and three nights. After that, you'll probably have to return to Faerie. Unless you have some other human protector lined up."

"No, there is only you," she said. "You are all I need, Alec."

I didn't like the sound of that. I suddenly felt as if I was being used for something more than she was telling me. I sat back in my seat and sighed.

Gloria might not be able to use her faerie wiles on Detective Frasier but I was sure she was deceiving me somehow. There was definitely more going on here than met the eye.

Great. Just great.

CHAPTER 9

WE DROVE OUT OF THE park and I got enough signal on my phone to call London. While it rang on the other end of the line, I glanced over at Gloria.

She was looking out the window, quietly watching the scenery roll by. I had no idea what was going through her mind. She was trouble, I knew that much, and I wanted to kick her out of the car and tell her she was on her own where the Greek vampires were concerned but now that I'd promised to protect her for three days, I had to do it.

Breaking a deal with a faerie had bad consequences. I'd probably end up trapped in the faerie realm forever and there would be nothing anyone could do about it. That seemed to be the usual punishment in the lore.

As soon as my call went through to the phone on the main desk of the building called *Mysterium Import & Export*, a magical process of identification would have kicked in and told the Society exactly who was on the other end of the line.

"Hello, Mr. Harbinger, how can I help you?" a male English-accented voice said in my ear. I didn't have to ask how he knew it was me calling. The Society's identification methods went beyond simple caller I.D.

"Hi," I said. "I need to speak to my father, Thomas Harbinger. Could you put me through to his office, please?"

There was a half-second pause before he said, "I'm afraid Mr. Harbinger isn't available at the moment. Can I take a message?"

"Do you know when he will be available? This is important."

"I'm afraid not, sir."

"Okay, then I'll leave a message. Tell him to contact me urgently. This is an emergency. You got that?"

"Yes, Mr. Harbinger. I'll get that message to your father's secretary right away."

"Wait a minute," I said. "Put me through to the secretary."

"Very well," he said.

The line went silent for a few seconds and then picked up by a man with an American accent. "Michael Chester speaking. How can I help you, Alec?"

"Are you my father's secretary?"

"Yes, I am."

"I need you to get a message to him urgently. Can you do that for me?"

There was a moment of silence and I wondered if the call had been cut off. Then Michael Chester said, "I can't do that at the moment, Alec."

"What? Why not? Look, if this is because he thinks I'm calling about the x-rays…"

"No, Alec." He let out a low sigh and said, "Your father is missing."

CHAPTER 10

WHAT DO YOU MEAN HE'S missing?"

Michael cleared his throat. "He disappeared four days ago. He wasn't even doing anything dangerous at the time, just going for lunch at The Swan, a pub near here where he eats regularly. He never arrived."

"What? Why didn't you tell me? You're looking for him, right? What have you turned up so far? There must be something."

"Of course we're looking for him. According to his driver, Thomas insisted on getting out of the car while they were driving through Hyde Park. He said there was something he had to do and that he'd be back shortly. Then he walked into the woods. The driver waited ten minutes before going to look for him. There was no sign of your father in the woods and no one has seen him since.

97

"We didn't inform you because the remaining members of the Inner Circle decided there was no need. They were going to handle this themselves and find him." He paused and then his voice took on a worried tone. "But that was days ago and they don't seem to be any closer to knowing where he is. I was going to call you, Alec, but I was under strict orders not to give out any information regarding your father's disappearance."

Anger rose within me. I should have been told about this the day he went missing, not four days later. Anything could have happened to him and the Inner Circle decided not to tell me?

"You're probably angry," Michael said, as if he could detect it over the phone line. "I don't blame you. And what I'm going to say next might make you angrier but I'm just telling you what's happening here, all right?"

"What is it?" I asked through gritted teeth, not sure I could get any angrier.

"There's talk," Michael said in a hushed tone, "of the Midnight Cabal. I've heard a rumor that your father may be a traitor, that he may have gone over to the Cabal willingly."

I was wrong; I *could* get angrier. The idea of my father betraying the Society he had dedicated his life to was unthinkable. Whoever was spreading those rumors needed to be stopped. "No one has given more of themselves to the Society than him," I told Michael.

"I know that," he agreed. "But you have to realize what we've been through lately. Traitors have been revealed at the highest levels. There are changes sweeping through the Society. It's only natural that when your father disappeared, the rumor surfaced that he was a Cabal member."

"I need to speak to someone in the Inner Circle," I said. "I have information I was going to pass on to my father but since he's not there, I have to give it to someone else."

"That would be Hans Lieben," Michael said. "He took over your father's duties shortly after he disappeared. Lieben is a member of the Inner Circle but I'm not sure I trust him, Alec." He lowered his voice to a whisper and added, "I'm not sure I trust anyone. Your father is a good man. It doesn't make sense that they're saying these things about him."

"Can you put me through to Lieben?"

"No, I can't do that. I'm just a lowly secretary as far as Lieben is concerned; he won't talk to me. The best I can do is to leave a message with his secretary, asking Lieben to contact you."

"Make sure you tell him it's urgent," I said.

"If I find out anything about your father's whereabouts, I'll let you know," he said before hanging up.

I took the phone from my ear and realized I was gripping it so tightly my knuckles were white. My father had dedicated his entire life to the Society of Shadows and there was no way he would defect to the Midnight Cabal. The members of the Inner Circle were crazy if they thought otherwise.

Unless someone was trying to discredit him. Maybe a Cabal member was using the current climate of fear to fan the flames of paranoia until they spread through the Society's headquarters like wildfire.

"Everything okay?" Leon asked, turning in his seat to face me.

"No, my dad has gone missing."

His face fell. "I'm sorry, man."

"Thanks. It sounds like there are search parties out looking for him but they haven't come up with anything yet."

"You think he was kidnapped?" Jim asked.

"I don't know."

"You going to fly over to England and look for him?"

"No, the Society has people searching for him and it has more resources than I could ever get my hands on. If anyone can find him, it's the Society. That's assuming he wants to be found."

"What do you mean?"

"Apparently, just before he vanished, he told his driver to stop the car and he wandered into the woods at Hyde Park, alone. If he was taken, his abductors would have to know he was going to get out of the car at that exact location and be there waiting for him. It sounds too implausible. Maybe he disappeared on purpose."

"Why would he do that?" Leon asked.

I shrugged. "I'm not sure. But the Society is in turmoil. My dad has been rooting out the traitors there. Maybe he needed to escape before he became the target of one of those traitors."

"It's possible," Jim said. "Your father is a clever man. He might have seen danger heading his way and disappeared to avoid it."

"Yeah," I said. "The problem is, who's left in charge of the Society? My dad's secretary mentioned a man named Hans Lieben. I've never heard of him. Have you?"

Jim shook his head. "No, I haven't. But we don't know the names of most of the Inner Circle members. Hans Lieben could be one of the good guys."

"Yeah, I know," I admitted. "It's just hard to know who to trust right now."

"I hear ya," Jim said, looking at me pointedly in the rearview mirror. I knew he was referring to Gloria.

Turning to her, I said, "Tell me more about these vampires."

She turned from the window and shrugged. "I've told you everything I know. They're trying to kill me because they want to take over my part of Faerie. My forest."

"You said they want something that only you know the location of. What is it?"

She sighed and waved me away, turning her attention back to the window. "That is no concern of yours."

"We're putting our lives on the line to help you protect this thing. We want to know what it is."

Gloria sighed as if frustrated. "Our bargain does not include the exchange of information. Your task is merely to protect me."

"That isn't the way I do things. I'm of more use to you if I know what these vampires want than if I'm fighting blind. And I don't like being put in situations where there's more going on than I'm being told."

Gloria turned to me and said, "You will escort me to where I need to go and protect me from the vampires and their demon minions. Our deal is as simple as that."

"Escort you? You didn't mention anything about that. You said protect you."

She nodded. "Yes, protect me while I go where I need to go."

"And where is that?"

"If I am to take back my forest from the Midnight Cabal, I need the item I told you about. You will escort me to it and protect me from harm while I return to Faerie and use it on those disgusting demons that have invaded my forest."

I looked at her closely. "So you're not running at all. You're preparing for a counter-attack and you're dragging me along to fight for you."

"You will be my hero," she said, "and they will sing songs about you in Faerie for all eternity." She touched my arm and I felt a warmth flicker from her fingers and travel along my skin. The tattoo on my shoulder heated up.

"I told you to stop with the glamor crap."

She removed her hand. "I'm sorry. But you really will be a hero and the faerie bards really will compose songs about you." She turned to Leon and Jim. "About all of you."

"I want to know exactly where we're going and what the item is," I said.

"No, that isn't how these bargains work. You simply do as I ask."

"That may be the way things are done normally but that isn't how I operate, especially when my friends' lives are on the line. Either you tell us what it is we're escorting you to, or the deal is off."

Her eyes flared an angry dark blue hue for a brief second before returning to their normal icy color. "Our deal is not off. Do you know the consequences of breaking a bargain with a faerie, especially one as powerful as me? You will be taken to my realm and kept there for all eternity."

"Maybe I will but you'll be trapped in a dungeon somewhere being tortured by vampires and demons, because I won't protect you from them unless you tell me exactly what's going on."

She balled her hands into fists and slapped them down on her thighs. "Ugh! You humans are so frustrating!" She sighed melodramatically and rolled her eyes up toward the ceiling of the Jeep. "Very well. I need you to help me get my torc."

"Your torc?"

"Yes, it's a circlet of gold. Mine is beautiful, decorated with carvings of acorns, leaves, rubies, and jade."

"I know what a torc is. So why is this one so important and how is it going to help you take back your forest?"

She sighed as if the answer to my question should have been obvious. "All faerie queens possess a torc. When worn around the neck, it allows us to draw on the power of the land. Each torc represents the queen's connection to her part of the faerie realm."

"And yours is hidden somewhere?"

"They are all hidden. They are too powerful to wear all the time so each queen hides her torc somewhere safe, somewhere hidden from her enemies. I hid mine here, in your world."

I nodded, understanding. "So the Midnight Cabal wants to steal your torc and take over your part of the realm."

"Yes. They want to imprison me and use my power, through the torc, to rule my land. They've already done so in other parts of Faerie. My sister, the Lady of the Mountains, is also in danger. I wanted to warn her that the creatures who destroyed my forest will be heading for her mountains next but I had no time. I had to escape. I only hope she's all right." An expression of genuine sadness passed over her features and her eyes looked down at her hands as she pondered her sister's fate. "Retrieving the torc is my only hope of returning home."

I actually felt a little sorry for her. Her forest had been occupied by monsters and for all she knew, her sister might also be exiled, or even dead. Gloria was a long way from home, putting her life in my hands while she was on the run.

"Don't worry," I told her, "we'll escort you to the torc and help you get your forest back." We might also destroy the Midnight Cabal's plans to use Faerie as a base of operations. Helping Gloria might allow us to strike at the Cabal before they could start the war they seemed intent on fighting against the Society.

Gloria's sorrow became a smile. "Thank you, Alec. You are my hero." She looked around the car at Leon, Jim, and then back to me. "All of you are my heroes."

"I can live with that," Leon said.

I looked out of the window at the trees rolling by. I could live with being a hero, I just didn't want to be a dead one.

CHAPTER 11

FELICITY WAS GOING MAD WITH worry. She had no idea if Alec was alive or dead and she couldn't think of anything else. She sat in the window seat of her parents' library, looking out at the garden she'd played in as a child and the sunny Sussex countryside beyond the far-off hedge, telling herself that Alec was fine and the only reason he hadn't rung was because he was in an area where his phone didn't work.

She sighed and got up from the seat, pacing back and forth on the library's oak floor, between the stacks of leather-bound books that looked down at her impassively. She'd loved these books as a child and had spent many hours in the leather armchair by the fireplace, studying the illustrations of far-away countries and intriguing relics that had been unearthed from a mysterious past.

Many of the books concerned the ancient Egyptians, her parents' field of expertise, but some of the tomes were concerned with other ancient cultures and had taught Felicity about the Romans, Greeks, Minoans, and Macedonians.

She knew precise details of long-forgotten rituals and obscure nuances of lost languages, yet all she wanted to know at this moment was the answer to one simple question: was Alec all right?

The door opened and her father came into the library. He was dressed in dark trousers and a light shirt, the outfit he wore for most occasions—whether taking part in archeological digs or hosting dinner parties at the house—but the shirt hung loosely on his tall frame. He'd lost weight, a fact that was also evidenced in his pinched facial features. He looked like a man who had been to hell and back, and it hurt Felicity to see him like this.

He smiled when he saw her and said, "I thought I might find you here. This always was your favorite room in the house." He lowered himself into the leather armchair and sighed, as if the effort of coming in here from the next room had exhausted him.

"You should take it easy," she told him, worried about the tired look that had settled on her father's face.

"Nonsense. I'm supposed to do some light exercise every day, building up a bit at a time. I'm no use to anyone if I can't even walk around the house. I might as well be dead."

"Dad, don't talk like that."

"Well, it's true. You and your mother have been putting your own lives aside to look after me ever since I had this bloody heart attack. It's time I looked after myself." He looked at her closely. "Which is what I want to talk to you about."

"What do you mean?"

"I mean it's time you went back to America. Your mother tells me you've been on edge lately and I've noticed it myself. You want to get back to your job, the new life you're making for yourself. And I don't blame you. I appreciate everything you've done, Felicity, but I can't have you stuck here with me and your mum when you have a life of your own to lead. Besides," he said, offering her a weak smile, "I'm on the mend. I'll be back to my old self in no time. It isn't fair to keep you here. Your mum can do enough fussing around me for both of you."

"I don't mind being here, really, I don't," she said, crouching next to the chair and taking his hand. "I love you, Dad."

"And I love you. Which is why I want you to go back to America and live your life."

"In a couple of days, perhaps." She didn't want to leave until her dad was looking at least a little better. Besides, if she returned to Dearmont now, the office would be empty. Alec was still in Canada and she had no idea how long he'd be there.

There wouldn't be much of a job to do while Alec was gone. She could take phone calls, of course, and talk to prospective clients, but all she would be able to tell them was that the P.I. was away at the moment and would deal with their case when he returned. She might as well stay here with her parents.

Was that the real reason she was reluctant to return to Dearmont, though? She wasn't sure where she stood with Alec on a personal level and a small part of her wondered if she was using her father's heart attack as an excuse to stay in England and not have to face Alec and deal with what was going on between them.

She liked Alec a lot, but a few weeks ago, she had been ready to marry Jason. She'd realized at the last moment that it wasn't the life she'd wanted but didn't that prove her mind was all over the place? It felt wrong to start a relationship with Alec right now. And he was still trying to get over Mallory leaving him.

Mallory had told Alec she needed some space for a while and, at the moment, that was how Felicity felt too.

Jason had hurt her, not least in his attitude toward her job and independence. Felicity had no fear that Alec would ever hurt her like that—he was in a totally different league to Jason—but her emotions had been scraped raw and she needed time for them to heal over before she exposed them again to anyone.

What had happened between her and Alec wasn't a bad thing—in fact, it had been exciting—but the timing was just wrong.

"Well, don't feel you have to stay here because of me or your mother," her dad said. "We can manage just fine."

"I know," Felicity said, "but I don't mind staying here a bit longer. I like visiting, you know that."

He looked at her with a sadness in his eyes. "It's just a shame that every time you come, it's because of something bad. Last time, you split up with Jason and this time, it's because my bloody heart has been playing up. It would be nice to have you here under better circumstances."

"Yes," she agreed, "it would." Then, remembering the split with Jason and the phone call she'd received from her mother, telling her that her father had suffered a heart attack, she murmured, "There does always seem to be something bad happening."

"One of my colleagues rang the other day to see how I was getting on," her dad said. "He joked that I'd been researching Ancient Egyptian heart curses so much that I'd put a curse on myself. Absolute nonsense, of course, but it does have a certain irony to it."

"Heart curses?" she asked, her interest piqued.

He nodded. "A little-known practice that was taking place during the eighteenth dynasty. A priest would cut the heart out of someone who was presumed to have power and then seal it into an urn, or a chest, or some other such container. Then the receptacle was supposed to receive the power of the heart donor. It was called the Sealing of the Heart.

"Then, of course, a curse was written on the container, saying that if anyone destroyed the heart inside, a terrible fate would befall them. So the 'heart vessels' were untouched. Even grave robbers feared them. A few have been unearthed in their original state."

Felicity's mind began racing. "How could the curse be broken?"

Her father looked at her with an amused expression and shrugged. "I don't know. I expect there was some myth about it but I haven't come across it in my research yet. I'm writing an article for The British Museum. They're going to have an exhibition next year. Some of the vessels used to hold the hearts were quite beautiful."

Felicity thought of the Box of Midnight and its gold and silver panels inscribed with hieroglyphs. "Yes, I know. What source documents are you using?"

"Are you interested in the subject? Yes, of course you are. You were always interested in the lesser-known practices, and the Sealing of the Heart was quite obscure." He got to his feet and led Felicity to an old desk beneath the window at the far end of the room. The surface of the desk was covered with papers and books. "This is the material I'm sifting through," he said. "There are copies of some papyri there and this codex"—he tapped one of the books—"mentions the ritual."

"Do you mind if I look through them?" she asked.

"Of course not. If you find anything interesting for my article, let me know. I really should get back to work on that as soon as possible."

"You should rest," Felicity told him. "I'll go through this material and make notes of anything interesting. Then you can write it up later. Meanwhile, do what the doctor told you and take it easy for a couple of weeks."

He looked from Felicity to the desk, then back again. "I suppose you're right. It's a lovely day. I might sit out in the garden for a while. Care to join me?"

"You go ahead," she said. "I'll make a start on this." She indicated the papers and books.

He chuckled. "Same old Felicity, can't resist exploring the past. What are you looking for, anyway?"

"Nothing, I just find the subject interesting."

He gave her a knowing look. "You can't fool me. I know when you're on a treasure hunt. You have the same glint in your eyes as you had when you were a little girl and your mother and I hid Easter eggs around the house."

"I just want to have a look, that's all."

He grinned. "If you don't want to tell me, that's fine. I'll be in the garden if you need me." He patted her affectionately on the shoulder and made his way to the door. Once there, he turned and said, "Don't take too long. I'll get your mother to brew a pot of tea later. Come outside and enjoy it with us."

"All right, I will." She waited until he was gone and then seated herself at the desk. When she reached for the nearest stack of papers she noticed her hands shaking slightly. Adrenaline was pumping through her veins. She felt anxious and excited, and a bit nervous.

Somewhere on this desk might be a way to break the curse that had taken hold of Mallory.

CHAPTER 12

WE ARRIVED AT JIM'S HOUSE and got out of the Jeep. Before we went on whatever journey Gloria had in mind, I wanted us to take stock and plan ahead. There was no point blundering ahead unprepared, especially when we were going up against a pair of powerful vampires.

Also, I wanted to call Felicity and let her know we were okay and tell her about my father. I could update her on the current situation with Gloria and get her to do some research on Davos and Korax. If they'd been around for as long as Gloria seemed to think they had, there must be a record of them somewhere in the Society's database. Maybe there was some information that would give us an edge against them.

"You guys go ahead," I told the others as they were walking toward the house. "I'm going to call Felicity." I hit her name in the contacts list on my phone and paced back along the road as I waited for the call to connect. Felicity answered after a couple of rings.

"Alec, how are you? Is everything all right?"

"Everything's fine," I told her. "We killed the nightwing but the case has developed into much more than we originally thought."

"What do you mean?"

I told her about my father's disappearance, then about the appearance of the Lady of the Forest and my deal with her to retrieve her torc and take back the faerie forest from Davos and Korax.

"I'm sorry about your father and all this torc business sounds very dangerous," Felicity said when I was done.

"Yeah, it probably is," I agreed. "But I don't have any choice. Breaking a deal with a faerie queen is probably just as dangerous. So, I'm going to see it through and get free of my debt. At least that will be one less thing to worry about."

"I suppose so. Listen, Alec, I have some potentially good news. I don't want you to get your hopes up just yet but I've found some ancient Egyptian writings regarding heart curses."

"Heart curses? You mean like the curse Mallory picked up from that damned box?"

"Yes, the curse Rekhmire cast on the Box of Midnight. It's called a heart curse. It's mentioned in some of the codexes and there are references to it in hieroglyphs painted on the wall of Amenhotep's tomb. I've got photographs to work from."

A sudden flame of hope flickered to life inside me. "Do they mention a way to break the curse?"

"I haven't found anything yet but I'm still looking and there's a lot of material to read through."

"That's great."

"As I said, don't get your hopes up yet. I just thought I should let you know there's a chance. A glimmer of hope but nothing more than that at the moment."

"Still, it's something," I said. "I was going to ask you to see if you could find any information on Davos and Korax but now I think it's better if you follow your lead about the curse."

"I can do both," she said. "I have my laptop here. I'm making some notes for my dad for an article he's writing. I can log into the Society's database now and have a quick look."

I heard her fingers on the keyboard and then she said, "I'm in. I'll try Davos first and see what we…oh, that's strange."

"What's wrong?"

"Nothing. The screen just flickered for a second. The database disappeared and then came back. Just give me a moment." I heard her keyboard clacking again. "There's something here. Davos is one of three vampires thought to have originated on the island of Crete around 1500 B.C.

Alec, that's the time of the Minoans. He's been around since then?"

"Sounds like it," I said. I thought of all the vampires I'd fought. The oldest had been a female vamp in Chicago who was supposedly three hundred years old and she'd been damned hard to kill. Davos was over three thousand and he had a companion who was probably just as old. "Does it mention Korax?" I asked Felicity.

"Yes, it mentions him as one of Davos's known associates, along with a female vampire named Damalis. They all originated from Crete during the same time period. They must have seen the fall of the Minoan civilization. That's incredible."

"They were probably the cause of the fall of the Minoan civilization," I said. "Three vampires could wreak destruction on an island of primitive villages. They'd tear through the population like foxes in a henhouse."

"Yes, they could," she agreed. "No one is exactly sure how the Minoans were destroyed. Some historians say the nearby island of Thera erupted and the ash drifted over Crete. Others think the Mycenaeans invaded. If there were vampires on the island, that adds a new dimension to the theories, I suppose."

"Either way, we're facing ancient creatures," I said.

"Yes." Her tone was grim.

"I don't suppose the database tells us an easy way to defeat them?" I said.

"No. They're vampires, so the usual methods should work. Wooden stakes, beheading, or fire. The problem is, those methods will be more difficult to employ because these vampires will be stronger, faster, and probably more cunning than any you've encountered before."

"Did I mention they have demon minions?" I asked in a breezy tone, attempting to lighten the mood.

"No, you didn't. Alec, please be careful. I know I say that every time we speak but I wouldn't feel right if I didn't."

"I'll be careful," I told her.

"I have to go," she said. "My dad is tapping on the window. He wants me to go out and join him for tea."

"Okay, I'll call you later when I know more about what it is we have to do to get the faerie queen's torc."

"All right, I look forward to it."

"Take care, Felicity." I ended the call and walked back to the house to give everyone the bad news. The vampires we faced were monsters from ancient times and I had no idea how we were going to beat such powerful creatures to Gloria's torc and take the faerie forest from them.

In fact, I had no idea how we were going to stay alive.

CHAPTER 13

T HAT'S GREAT," JIM SAID AFTER I delivered the news. "Just great."

We were sitting around the picnic table, waiting for steaks to cook on the barbecue. The smell of sizzling meat drifted enticingly on the warm air, making my mouth water. We each had a bottle of beer on the table in front of us. Gloria hadn't touched hers but stared at it with a mixture of wonder and wariness.

"I told you we shouldn't get involved in this," I said to Jim. "You thought it'd be a good idea."

"Only because I wanted to help you pay off the debt you incurred in Faerie. Nobody mentioned ancient vampires."

"If you want to back out now, there are no hard feelings," I said.

He screwed up his eyes in disgust. "You know I'd never do that, Alec. I just don't like being played by this faerie. First she put dreams in my head to get you to come here and then she forgot to mention that the two vampires chasing her have been around since ancient times. It's typical faerie behavior and we fell for it."

"I'm sitting right here," Gloria said, still staring at her beer. "I can hear everything you're saying about me."

"Good," Jim said, leaning over the table toward her. "Maybe it's time you got a dose of truth. Humans aren't just playthings for you to manipulate when it suits you. We don't like being controlled."

"I haven't controlled anyone," Gloria said, looking at Jim. "You acted on the dreams of your own free will. I told you there were two vampires trying to capture me. You didn't ask me how old they were until later. I've done nothing wrong."

"What Jim's trying to say," Leon told Gloria, "is that maybe you should think about being more forthright from now on. We don't want any nasty surprises to bite us on the ass."

She looked at him, raised an eyebrow, and repeated, "I've done nothing wrong."

Jim shook his head, left the table, and went over to the barbecue. He began turning the steaks over and muttering to himself.

"Are you going to drink that beer or just stare at it?" I asked Gloria.

Her eyes widened and she returned her gaze to the beer in front of her. Condensation was sliding down the brown glass, pooling on the wooden table around the base of the bottle.

"I don't know," she said. "I have experienced so little of human food and drink that I'm not sure I'll like it."

"Only one way to find out," I said.

Gloria nodded and reached for the beer, bringing the mouth of the bottle to her lips and taking a tiny sip. She swallowed and smiled. "This tastes interesting." She took another swig, tipping her head back and draining the bottle.

"You might want to go easy with that," I said, "especially when you aren't used to it."

Putting the empty bottle on the table, she let out a little burp and laughed. "It's so delightful." She reached down to the cooler on the ground, rummaged around in it, and brought out another bottle.

"Like I said, go easy." I went over to the barbecue to join Jim. "You okay?" I asked him when I was by his side.

"Yeah, I'm good, Alec." He didn't look at me, choosing instead to watch the cooking meat. "It's just when I think of all the things we faced, all the times we saved each other's lives, it would be a shame if we get taken out of the game because a faerie tricked us."

I nodded. "I agree. Which is why we're going to survive this, just like we survived all those other things. If we have to kill a couple of ancient vampires along the way, then so be it."

He grinned. "You make it sound so easy."

I shrugged. "Maybe it will be. Maybe ancient vampires rely on their reputation to protect them from being attacked. Maybe they're actually weak and we'll kill them without breaking a sweat."

He laughed. "Yeah, I don't think so."

"Okay, so maybe we can get to Gloria's torc before the vampires catch up with us."

He nodded. "Yeah, maybe, but I doubt it." Using a meat fork, he took the steaks off the grill and put them onto a plate and gestured with his chin toward the faerie queen. "What do you think of her, Alec? What's with this 'Gloria' persona she's adopted?"

"I don't know. She's treating this more like a vacation than a life-threatening situation."

"Well, that could change if those vamps find us," Jim said. "Here, take these to the table while I get the salad from the kitchen."

I did so, taking my place next to Gloria. She looked at me with glassy eyes and grinned. There were now three empty bottles on the table in front of her.

I looked over at Leon. "Did she drink all these?"

He nodded. "Yeah, I told her to stop after the third but I think it was too late."

Gloria giggled. "I can see now why humans like to eat and drink so much. I don't have to eat at all, of course, because I'm a faerie, but I like this beer." She pointed with an unsteady hand at the three empties. "It's made me feel very relaxed." She sighed and looked up at the sky. "It's very nice here."

"I think it's time we introduced you to black coffee," I said, getting up and heading for the house. To Leon, I said, "Don't let her have any more beers."

"They're all gone," he said.

I went into the kitchen where Jim was supposed to be preparing the salad. But instead of doing that, he was standing stock still in the middle of the room, his face upturned slightly. It looked like he was listening to something.

I stopped and listened too. Apart from the hum of the refrigerator, the ticking of the kitchen clock, and the sounds of Leon and Gloria talking outside, I couldn't hear anything.

Jim held up a hand, telling me not to interrupt him. After a minute passed, marked out by sixty ticks of the clock on the wall, he said, "Someone's coming. They've passed the wards on the road."

So he hadn't been listening at all, he'd been mentally connecting to the wards. Because he lived in a remote area, Jim had placed wards on the road approaching the house. They were low-level, so they didn't keep out intruders but alerted Jim when anyone with ill-intent went past them.

I'd considered casting similar wards at the end of my street in Dearmont but the problem with such protection spells was that they had a loose interpretation of "ill intent." So, if one of my neighbors decided he didn't like the guy with the Land Rover and the lawn that sometimes went too long without being mowed, the ward would activate every time that neighbor drove onto the street.

So I kept my wards around the house itself. It meant I didn't have an early warning system if someone actually meaning to do me harm was approaching my house but it also meant I wouldn't get an unsettling feeling in my gut every time the guy who lived across the road came home from work.

Another advantage Jim had, living out in the woods, was that he could keep a weapon rack in his living room without having to worry that it might be seen by the local Jehovah's Witnesses or a Girl Scout selling cookies.

We went to the weapon rack and we each took a sword from it. I grabbed one for Leon, too. We also picked up a crossbow and a quiver of bolts each.

I opened the screen door and shouted, "Leon, get the shotgun from the Jeep." Without a second's hesitation, he ran for the vehicle and opened the trunk.

Jim and I took the weapons to the picnic table and strapped the swords to our belts. When we were armed, and Leon had come back with the shotgun, I looked at Gloria. "Someone's coming this way. Jim's wards flared into life, so it's someone looking for trouble."

She blinked against the sun as if it were too bright. "We should get out of here." Clambering to her feet, she pointed dramatically at the Jeep and Explorer. "Quickly, to the vehicles." Then she took a couple of steps forward before falling to the ground and lying there, laughing.

Leon looked down at her, then at me. "Wow, she really can't hold her liquor."

For a moment, I considered bundling her into the trunk of one of the vehicles. At least she'd be out of our way.

We waited, standing in the mid-afternoon heat, hands on the hilts of our swords, ready to draw them at the first sign of trouble.

"You hear that?" Leon whispered.

"What?" I asked. All I could hear was Gloria rolling around on the ground, giggling to herself.

"A car," Leon said.

"I hear it too," Jim said.

Gloria scrambled to her feet and sat down at the picnic table again. "That wasn't a good idea. I'll just stay right here."

The sound of the car got louder as the vehicle got closer. When it came into view and parked at the side of the house, I let out a relieved sigh. It was the green Chevy Tahoe that Frasier and Girard drove.

The two detectives got out of the vehicle and came across the lawn toward us. There was a purposeful determination in Girard's stride but his face was unreadable.

"Well, that explains the wards," Jim said. "Girard has never liked me." He put on a false smile and said to Girard, "How can I help you, detective?"

"Cut the crap, Walker. If you know something about those killings, I want to hear it."

Jim shrugged. "I thought you didn't believe in monsters?"

"Oh, I believe in monsters," Girard said, "I've met plenty of them. And every one of them was human. Now, if you know who killed those people on the trails, I want that information. Otherwise, I'm going to arrest you and your friends here for obstructing a peace officer."

"That term doesn't apply to you," Jim said. "You aren't exactly a peaceful guy, Girard."

"Says the guy with a sword strapped to his belt. What the hell is going on here, anyway? Some kind of role-playing?"

"It isn't any of your business," Jim said.

Girard went up to Jim and stood in front of him, hands on hips, his sports jacket open just enough to show the butt of his sidearm. "I'll tell you what is my business, Walker: murder. This is a murder case and you can't just declare it solved and expect us to forget about it. Who's the murderer? Where's the evidence?"

"You want to see the evidence? I'll show you on a map where it is. You can see for yourself."

Girard snorted. "I'm not going into the backcountry to look for Bigfoot, so forget about it. I want answers here and now. So start talking."

"Like I told you, Girard..." Jim stopped, his voice fading away. He held up a hand as if telling everyone to be quiet. Everyone complied, even Girard. After a couple of seconds, Jim said, "The wards. Something just went past them."

"Don't try to pull that crap on me," Girard said. "We're going to sit down and you're going to tell me what you know about this murder case. I don't want to hear about flying monsters, ghosts, or trolls. And I..." He paused, turning his attention to the house and the woods beyond. "What's that noise?"

I heard it too, a rustling coming through the trees, as if dozens of people were rushing through the woods toward the house.

Gloria, who had been sitting quietly at the table, looked up with fearful eyes and said, "They're here."

CHAPTER 14

THEY CAME SWARMING OVER THE roof of Jim's house, dozens of red-skinned demons with hatred burning in their flame-yellow eyes. Some of them had horns, some flew on bat-like wings. All of them brandished weapons: axes, swords, wickedly-spiked maces, and cruel-looking whips.

I loaded my crossbow. I couldn't see how we could win against so many of them but wasn't going down without a fight.

Girard stared open-mouthed and wide-eyed at the demonic invaders and muttered. "What. The. Fuck?" His hand went to his gun and he fumbled it from its holster with shaking hands.

Frasier seemed less perturbed than Girard and was already crouching in a firing stance, her gun held steady in both hands.

From the corner of my eye, I saw Leon bring the shotgun up to his shoulder, then heard the loud report as he pulled the trigger. A demon that had been crawling down the side of the house dropped to the ground.

The noise seemed to shock Girard awake. He began firing indiscriminately at the demons, his eyes still wide with disbelief.

I loosed a bolt at a winged demon that was swooping toward us and caught it in the neck, sending it spinning into the wall of the house. It slid down the wall and lay dead by the porch steps.

The stench of sulfur filled the air. It invaded my lungs and made me want to puke, but I held it together and fired at a second demon, this one dashing across the lawn toward Gloria. The bolt pierced its chest and the demon stumbled before sprawling on the grass. It landed at Frasier's feet and she put a bullet through its head to make sure it was dead.

"There are too many of them!" Jim shouted. "We need to get out of here!"

We made a dash for the vehicles. I abandoned the crossbow and drew my sword, its blue glow lighting the air around me. I looked over at Gloria, who was standing by the table and watching the demons swarm over the house, and told her, "Get behind me. Stay with me."

She nodded and came over to me, weaving slightly.

I pointed at the Explorer. "We're going that way." I stepped forward as a tall, heavily-muscled demon approached with a hand ax. It swung it at me and I ducked, hearing the blade whistle through the air above my head. I lunged forward and drove my sword into its belly. The demon roared in pain. I used my boot to kick him backward into one of his companions, freeing my sword so I could swing it at a winged demon that seemed hell-bent on catching Gloria. It swooped down to grab her as I swung the blade up at its body.

The blade bit into the demon's side and lodged between its ribs. I arced the sword, with the demon still attached, over my head and toward the table, slamming the winged creature through the wood. The picnic table splintered, empty bottles smashing into each other, the steaks landing on top of the dead demon's body.

I removed my sword from its body and made a dash for the Explorer. Gloria was ahead of me, staggering toward the vehicle. She tripped and went sprawling headlong into the dirt. She cried out and I wasn't sure if it was from pain or fear.

One of the demons on the roof took the opportunity to leap down beside her and scoop her into its arms. It glared at me with a look of triumphant hatred and grinned.

Then its head jerked back and the demon fell to the ground, Gloria scrambling out of its arms.

Frasier appeared beside me, reloading her gun.

"Good shot," I said.

"We can discuss marksmanship later," she replied, aiming her newly-loaded weapon at a demon by the Jeep and taking it down with a head shot. She walked steadily over to the Jeep, gun raised to eye level and held in both hands.

Gloria was opening the door of the Explorer, clambering onto the back seat. I ran over, slid behind the wheel, and started the engine. As it roared to life, I looked back at the melee by the house.

Leon was sprinting for the Explorer, shotgun discarded and sword in hand. I leaned across and opened the passenger door for him. Jim was heading for the Jeep, where Frasier was already in the passenger seat and shooting out of the window. Girard was close behind Leon, turning every so often to fire at the mass of red bodies swarming from the lawn toward the vehicles.

I heard the Jeep's engine start and then Jim backed away from the house, swinging the vehicle in a tight arc so it pointed at the road. Frasier was still firing from the passenger-side window, blowing away demons with expert precision.

Leon got in next to me, breathing hard. "Let's go," he panted.

"We've got one more passenger to collect," I said, gesturing to Girard.

The detective was on one knee, picking his targets from the horde of demons and taking them down with steady, controlled shots.

"Girard, move your ass!" I shouted at him.

He didn't seem to hear me and I wasn't sure if that was because he was too far away or because he was in shock. The appearance of the demons had shattered his worldview; a worldview that he'd seemed to believe in unwaveringly. He'd just been shown that the preternatural world he'd denied so strongly was real. His mind would take some time to adjust to this new reality.

I slammed the Explorer into reverse and spun the wheel so we swung back to where Girard was fighting the creatures he'd refused to believe in for so long.

Gloria opened the door for Girard and he jumped into the vehicle, panting for breath. "I got some of them. Maybe a dozen. I don't…I don't know what they are."

"They're demons," I told him as I put the Explorer into gear and pushed the accelerator pedal all the way down, shooting us forward onto the road. "They're here because they want to capture Gloria. She's a faerie queen. The demons want to take her to their masters, who are vampires from ancient Greece." Hell, he'd come this far, there was no reason not to tell him the whole truth.

He removed his shades and looked at Gloria.

She smiled at him drunkenly.

Girard frowned, processing what I'd just told him. Only a few minutes ago, before the demon attack, he would have scoffed at me and come up with a comment about how dumb I was for believing in such things.

Now, he just nodded thoughtfully and said, "Okay."

CHAPTER 15

"THEY'RE STILL COMING," I SAID, looking in the rearview and seeing a mass of crimson-skinned bodies chasing us. Some were running along the road while others flew among the trees.

Jim's Jeep was thirty feet ahead of us. Detective Frasier was attempting to hang out of the window and shoot past us at the demons but the road was so narrow, the trees so close on either side, that she had to keep pulling her head and arm back into the vehicle to avoid getting splattered against a tree trunk.

"What are we going to do?" Leon asked.

"They won't follow us all the way to town. We'll just have to outrun them."

Something landed on the roof of the Explorer with a heavy thud.

"I don't think that's an option," Leon said.

"I got this," Girard said, picking up my sword from the floor and stabbing it up through the roof. The enchanted blade went through the metal as if it were butter and, judging by the shriek of pain that came from outside, it also sliced through demon flesh.

When he brought the glowing blade back through the slit in the roof, Girard was grinning. "Wow, I've always wanted to do that."

"Then you can explain it to the rental company," I told him.

The winged demon that had been on the roof was brushed off by a low-hanging branch. It tumbled onto the road behind us and the running horde trampled over its body.

There was another thump on the roof. Girard eagerly thrust the sword up through the roof again but this time there was no sound on the other side. The demon leaped onto the Explorer's hood and glared through the windshield at us.

I tapped the brakes, attempting to shake it off, but even though we were all slammed against our seatbelts, the demon had its claws dug into the hood and remained in place.

The people at Hertz were going to have dollar signs in their eyes when I took the Explorer back.

The demon lunged at me, its deadly talons smashing through the windshield and cutting the air in front of my face.

I dodged the attack, slamming myself against the door, struggling with the wheel while trying to see past the demon's bulky body at the road beyond.

Leon reacted with lightning speed, thrusting his sword into the demon's belly. The creature howled and toppled into the trees, its black blood spurting over the Explorer's hood.

Ahead, Jim was approaching a fork in the road. He put his blinkers on to let me know he was going to take the right fork, the road that led to Huntsville, but Gloria shoved her face between the front seats and said, "Tell him to go left."

"What?"

She pointed at the Jeep. "He's going the wrong way."

"What are you talking about?"

"We need to go that way," she said, pointing at the road that led deeper into the woods.

"No, we don't. We need to get to town."

"We'll never make it." She looked at me. "Trust me. There's a portal in the woods ahead. I can sense it. We can use it to escape."

"A portal to where?"

"To Faerie, of course," she said, as if I were stupid to ask such a question.

135

"You just escaped from Faerie. Why would you want to go back there?"

She frowned at me as if I had just asked the dumbest question in the word. "Because we're being chased be demons."

I wasn't sure I could trust her. Reaching town seemed like our best option and heading deeper into the woods could get us killed. But then I smelled burning metal and realized we weren't going to make it to Huntsville anyway.

The demon's black blood was corroding the hood, eating its way down to the engine. The Explorer didn't have long left.

"Damn it!" The decision was made for me. I honked the horn and flashed my lights at the Jeep and pointed at the left fork. Without question, Jim turned onto the road that led into the woods.

"You'd better be right about this," I told Gloria.

"Don't worry," she said, closing her eyes. "The portal is close. I can feel it."

It had better be, because once that acidic demon blood reached the engine, we were screwed.

I reached the fork and followed Jim along the road that led away from Huntsville and wound through the woods. The demons chasing us on foot seemed to have inexhaustible energy, still running along the road.

Luckily, they didn't have superhuman—or super-demon— speed; they could keep up with the Explorer on the narrow, windy road where I couldn't put my foot down, but they couldn't catch up with us. There must have been at least fifty of them back there and if they managed to reach us, we were dead, no doubt about it.

The winged variety was faster and two of them swooped down onto the Explorer right after we passed the fork in the road. One of them landed on the roof, the other on the hood, obscuring my view of the road ahead.

"Girard," I said.

He thrust the sword up through the roof but the blade didn't seem to connect with anything. Girard peered up through the slits he'd cut in the roof. "Damn thing flew up to avoid the sword."

The creature on the hood lunged in at me through the shattered windshield. I instinctively raised an arm and punched it in the face, stunning it for a second; all the time Leon needed to run it through with his sword. The demon's hateful yellow eyes bulged as the enchanted blade slid into its body. Leon pulled the sword back out and I shoved at the dying creature, sending it toppling off the hood.

There was a thud when the demon that had flown upward to avoid Girard's attack landed on the roof again. Its talons punctured the roof, reaching down and clawing at the air over the back seat.

Gloria shrank back, a look of terror in her eyes.

Girard unholstered his gun and calmly shot up at the creature.

The sound was deafening, making my ears ring, but the demon fell dead onto the road behind us. Girard turned in his seat to shout triumphantly at the dead demon through the rear window, "Take that, you demonic bastard!" He turned back and pumped his fist, giving Gloria a grin.

She looked like she wasn't sure what to make of his behavior, returning his wide grin with a weak smile.

She said something to me but my hearing was still muffled, as if my ears were stuffed with cotton. I adjusted the rearview so I could see her in it and shouted, "What?"

"I said we need to stop here. The portal is that way." She pointed beyond Girard, through his side window.

"How far?" I asked her. "If we stop, those demons are going to catch up with us pretty soon."

"I'm sure it's close," she said.

That didn't fill me with confidence but the dark smoke that was beginning to plume into the air from beneath the hood told me we weren't going to be going much farther anyway. I flashed the Jeep and hit the brakes. The Explorer skidded to a stop. "Everybody out," I said.

We threw open the doors and scrambled out of the vehicle. The Jeep's brake lights came on and it slewed to a stop before Jim and Frasier got out. Jim ran around to the trunk and opened it, taking out the backpacks we'd stowed there earlier, as well as extra weapons he kept in there.

Running toward him, I shouted, "There's a portal to Faerie somewhere nearby."

He nodded and threw me a backpack and a sword. I hooked the backpack over my shoulder while running into the woods, following Gloria, who seemed to know where she was headed.

Girard and Leon were at her side, clutching their swords and flanking her as if they were two knights protecting a queen, which, I guessed, wasn't too far from the truth.

Jim, Frasier, and I ran to keep up with them. Frasier, smaller-framed and lighter than Jim and me, pumped her arms and legs like a professional runner, her gun gripped tightly in her left hand. There was a look of grim determination on her face and I wondered if she was thinking of her family and how much she wanted to return to them.

She and Girard had only come out to Jim's house to question him, probably at Girard's insistence, about the murder case and now they were running for their lives from demons. As a cop, Frasier obviously accepted certain dangers in her line of work but I was sure she'd never included fleeing from a demonic horde among her occupational hazards.

The demons on the road veered into the woods, crashing through the undergrowth. At least the trees were so close together here that the winged demons couldn't swoop down on us from above. They were effectively grounded.

Up ahead, I saw Gloria point at something and she, Leon, and Girard made for it. Jim, Frasier, and I adjusted our trajectory so we could get to whatever Gloria had pointed at as quickly as possible. And we needed to be quick because the demons were gaining on us. They increased their pace, as if sensing that we had an escape route somewhere ahead.

I used my sword to cut my way through a tangle of low-hanging branches and found Gloria standing in the center of a ring of hawthorn bushes, still flanked by her protectors.

"Quickly!" she urged when she saw me.

I ran into the circle, closely followed by Detective Frasier and Jim.

When we were all encircled by the hawthorn, Gloria said, "When the ground begins to glow, cut down some of the bushes. It'll break the circle so they won't be able to follow us." She closed her eyes and tilted her chin upward, chanting something under her breath.

The demons were no more than twenty feet away now, their eyes full of hatred and triumph. They thought they'd caught us.

The ground beneath our feet began to glow bright white and I slashed my sword at the closest bush, cutting it down with one blow.

There was a low hum of magical energy in the air all around us. It increased in pitch as the glow increased in intensity.

Then the woods and the demons disappeared and all that was left was a blinding white light.

CHAPTER 16

FELICITY SAT IN HER PARENTS' library, staring at a black-and-white photograph that had been taken in Egypt, in the tomb of Amenhotep II. The subject of the photo was a painting on the wall of the tomb that showed a man with a heart in his hand, standing before a mummy that had a hole in its chest. Between them was an open box.

The photo had been taken in 1963 but the painting was referred to in an older source. One of the leather-bound books on the desk, a historical text called *Wonders of the Tombs* by a man named Walpole, written in 1932, described the painting as: *The Sealing of the Heart. A priest removes a heart and places it inside a magical box.*

Felicity placed the photo next to the open book and searched through the other photos on the desk, looking for anything else that related to the Sealing of the Heart ritual. There were dozens of photographs, documenting thousands of hieroglyphs that had been painted on the wall of Amenhotep's resting place. It would take her weeks to go through all the material and there was no guarantee that any of the other hieroglyphs even mentioned the Sealing of the Heart or the curse that was placed on the magical vessels once the heart was sealed inside.

"Felicity, are you coming out for a while?"

Felicity turned in her seat to see her mother standing in the doorway with a tray of cups, saucers and a teapot.

"Yes, I'm coming," Felicity said, getting out of the chair and taking the tray from her mother. "Here, let me take those." She led the way out through the kitchen to the patio area where her father sat waiting at the garden table.

The dull evening light in the garden made Felicity realize she'd been sitting in the gloomy library for longer than she'd thought.

"You said you were coming out here hours ago," her dad said. "Got caught up in the research, eh?"

"Yes," she said, placing the tray on the table. "You know what I'm like when I get lost in a book."

"Well, let me tell you one thing this heart attack has taught me," he said as she took the chair next to him. "There's more to life than studying books about the people of history. You need to be concerned about the people in the present as well, the people right here, right now."

"Well, that's rich coming from you," her mother said. "You spent most of your life with your nose buried in a book, and now you're telling Felicity not to do the same just because you've come to some sort of epiphany?"

"I didn't say there isn't value in it," he countered, "just that there's no need to spend so much time doing it. It's important, of course, but those old texts can draw you in, make you forget about the real world. It becomes the most important thing in your life. But you need to look at it in perspective. It isn't as if learning about the Sealing of the Heart ritual is a life-or-death situation, is it?"

Felicity said nothing and watched her mother pour the tea. She couldn't tell him that learning about the ritual, particularly how to break the curse attached to it, could mean the difference between life and death for Alec's friend Mallory.

It was funny how she always thought of Mallory as Alec's friend and not as her own. She supposed she didn't really know the girl well enough to call her anything other than "Alec's friend." Every time she'd met Mallory, she'd sensed a barrier between them, a wall that neither of them seemed willing to break through.

She was at least partly responsible for the erection of that wall, she knew, and that was because she envied Mallory her close relationship with Alec. There was some kind of bond between them that was like nothing Felicity had ever experienced herself.

She wasn't even sure if she was jealous of the fact that Mallory had that bond with Alec, or if she was just jealous of the bond itself. She'd never felt such a deep connection to anyone. Her relationship with Jason had turned out to be so shallow that it could almost be called a business arrangement rather than a relationship.

"Ignore your father," her mother said. "He's in one of his philosophical moods."

Felicity smiled and took a sip of the hot tea. It burned her mouth but it tasted good. "I know what he's like," she said, "but he seems to be forgetting that my research is going to help him with his article for the British Museum."

Her mother looked at her husband with disapproval in her eyes. "You asked Felicity to research your article for you?"

He looked up from his tea. "What? No, she offered. She's just collecting some information. It isn't as if I don't already know the subject backwards. A priest rips the heart from a living victim, puts it in a box or urn, says some magical words over it, and hey—presto, the bloody thing is regarded as an item of power. Then there's a curse put on it. The curse was a safeguard to make sure nobody opened up the vessel to find that the heart, instead of still beating as the legend said, was actually dead and shriveled up."

Felicity, who had been raising her cup to her mouth, froze for a second before putting the cup back down on the saucer. Something her father had just said struck a chord. A living victim. A still-beating heart.

"Felicity?' her mother asked. "Are you all right? You're staring into space."

"How could I be so bloody stupid?" Felicity muttered. "I knew the heart was taken from a living person but I didn't think of that when I saw the painting on the tomb wall."

She pushed back from the table and stood up. Her mother looked at her with worry in her eyes.

"Walpole was wrong," Felicity said, feeling a glimmer of hope. "He was bloody wrong." She ran back into the house.

When she was in the kitchen, she heard her father say, "See, this is what I mean. Too much research addles your brain."

She crossed the library to the desk and picked up the photo next to *Wonders of the Tombs*. Walpole's description of the painting on the tomb wall had been wrong. The priest wasn't taking a heart from a victim. He was standing before a mummy. A living heart was required for the sealing ritual, so this painting could not be of a priest taking a heart to seal it in the box at his feet.

Felicity studied the photograph. There was only one other interpretation: the priest had taken the heart out of the box and was putting it back into the mummy.

Was this the way to break the curse?

Her mind raced. The heart inside the Box of Midnight had been taken from a sorceress named Tia, a member of

Amenhotep II's court. So where was her mummy? Did it still exist?

She went to the shelves where her parents kept boxes containing research on Egyptian tombs. The sixty-three known tombs in the Valley of the Kings were coded from KV1 to KV63, and the boxes were labeled accordingly. She tried to remember which one was Amenhotep II's tomb. KV35, she was sure of it. She had to know if there were any mummies found in that tomb that might be Tia, and if so, where they were now.

She pulled the box from the shelf and set it on the floor before removing the cardboard lid and delving inside. There were photographs, research papers, and her parents' own writings on the pharaoh's tomb.

Her father appeared at the doorway, smiling. "Looks like you've got a bee in your bonnet about something."

"Tia," she said. "The sorceress who was killed by Rekhmire. Was she buried with Amenhotep II?"

"Are you talking about the legends?"

"What do you mean? What legends?" She continued sifting through the photos in the box.

"Well, the legends say that Rekhmire had Tia's body mummified and then hid it. And, of course, Rekhmire's own tomb has no burial chamber at all. It was built during his lifetime but he was never buried there. He fell out of favor with the royal court.

"The legends say he raised an army of the dead and marched on Amenhotep but that's obviously a more dramatic way of saying he built a regular army and tried to gain power. The ancient Egyptians were marvelous at inventing stories around mundane events and making them seem more dramatic."

Felicity replaced the photos in the box. If Rekhmire had taken Tia's mummy away and hidden it, there would be no clues to its whereabouts here. She felt suddenly deflated. Her discovery was meaningless if Tia's mummy was lost beneath the sands of time.

Her father looked at her with kindness and concern. "What's the matter? You look like you've got the weight of the world on your shoulders."

"It's nothing," she said. "I just thought I might find something that could help a friend of mine."

He grinned, a mischievous twinkle in his eyes. "Would that friend happen to be the man you work for? Alec Harbinger?"

"Yes, that's right. But I don't know why you're looking at me like that. He's my boss, nothing more."

Her father nodded slowly. "All right, if that's what you want to believe. But you should see the way your face lights up every time you speak about him. I may have a bad heart but there's nothing wrong with my eyes and I can see what's going on, you know."

Felicity felt her face heat up. "It really isn't like that," she protested weakly. She wasn't sure why she thought the words would fool her father; even as she said them, she didn't believe them herself.

"All right, I won't bring the subject up again. I can see it makes you uncomfortable. Just tell me this for my own peace of mind. Is he a good man, this Alec Harbinger?"

"Yes," she said, "he is."

"Then that's good enough for me. Between you and me, I wasn't all that keen on Jason. He seemed like the type of person who wouldn't do anything for anybody unless there was something in it for him."

"Alec isn't like that at all. Just the opposite, in fact. He'll do anything to help people, even if it means putting himself in danger."

"Danger?" Her father's eyes grew worried. "Felicity, please tell me you aren't doing anything dangerous."

She thought of the changelings, demons, and frog-monsters she'd faced. She couldn't bring herself to lie to her father, so she simply said, "You don't have to worry about me. I'm a grown woman."

He sighed in resignation. "You've always been strong-willed, so I know you'll do what you want, no matter what I say. All I ask is that you please be careful."

She smiled. It was the same thing she said to Alec every time he was about to embark on a new case. Now she knew where she'd picked up the sentiment.

"Always," she told her father, giving him one of the stock answers Alec sometimes gave her. Putting the box back on the shelf, she said, "I've done enough research for one day. I'll get back to it tomorrow."

He nodded. "No need to stress over it. Look at it with fresh eyes in the morning. Come and have something to eat, take your mind off those dusty old manuscripts for a while."

"I'll be there in a minute. I just want to ring Alec first and make sure he's all right."

When her father had left the room, she picked up her phone and called Alec. It went straight to voicemail. Felicity didn't leave a message.

She ended the call and stood quietly for a moment in the library, feeling an icy tendril of dread crawl up the back of her neck. She knew she shouldn't be so concerned just because Alec hadn't answered his phone. There were a million reasons why he might not be able to take her call. But, still, Felicity felt certain that something was wrong.

Beyond the window, the afternoon light had darkened and twilight had fallen. Felicity felt as if that darkness were weighing down on her, smothering her.

She was sure that Alec was in danger and she was also sure that he was far away, somewhere where she would never be able to reach him.

CHAPTER 17

THE BRIGHTNESS FADED AND THE world around me came into view. At first, I could only see the outlines of trees, then the clearing I was standing in, then the ring of hawthorn bushes around me. I looked around to see my friends standing with me.

"What the hell just happened?" Girard asked, pointing his gun at the surrounding forest. "Where are the demons?"

"We're in Faerie," I told him. "They can't follow us here. For now, anyway." I turned to Gloria. "Do you know exactly where we are?"

She looked at the trees, at the bright sky, and shook her head. "Not exactly, no."

"But we're in Faerie, right?"

Gloria nodded. "Oh, yes, definitely. But Faerie is a big place, at least as large as your world, probably even larger. I don't know every corner of it. I usually stay in my forest. And this…"—she gestured at the trees—"…is not my forest."

I turned to the others. "Listen to me carefully. Faerie is a dangerous place. Don't eat or drink anything, don't talk to the inhabitants, don't even look at anything for too long in case you become entranced."

"Oh, Alec," Gloria said, "you make it sound so dreadful. This is my home and the folk who live here aren't monsters."

"Some of them are," I told her. "Ogres, trolls, goblins…"

"Yes, yes, all right. No place is perfect."

"And whatever you do," I said to the others, "don't make a bargain with anyone here, no matter how innocent it might seem. You've all heard fairy tales where humans get stuck in the faerie realm, right?"

They nodded.

"They're true. Those stories were written as a warning and as a guide for dealing with faerie beings. Don't underestimate this place, because if you do, you'll never go home."

I looked around at them all in turn, trying to gauge if my words had sunk in. Jim had a look of grim determination on his face. He'd been here before and knew the risks. Leon looked similarly grim-faced. The last time we'd been here, he'd almost been entranced by two faeries in a pool so he knew to be on his guard. Detective Frasier looked worried as hell and I couldn't blame her for that. I was worried myself. Girard was looking around with a sense of wonder in his eyes, his face slack-jawed.

"Girard, pull it together," I told him. "If you let this place enchant you, it will."

He looked at me with dull, confused eyes. "Yeah, okay. I'm…fine."

I turned to Gloria. "How do we get out of here as quickly as possible and get back to the human world? You said that's where you hid your torc, so we're wasting time here."

"Yes, we need to go to your world," she said, "but it isn't as easy as that. First we need to find the right portal."

I sighed in frustration. I didn't want us spending any more time in Faerie than we had to, especially searching for another damned portal. Girard looked like he was losing it big time. He'd had a shock that had rocked his deepest beliefs. He wouldn't just get over that in a few days; it would take months, if not years.

"Gloria, the last time I was here, you opened up a portal with your magic. You didn't need a ring of stones or bushes. You just did it. So do it now."

"I can't. That was in my forest and those horrid vampires and demons hadn't come to take it over yet. You don't understand how much power I've lost simply by having my land taken away from me. That's why I need my torc. Without it, I'm just a has-been." She pouted and stomped her foot on the ground in frustration.

This was no time for drama. "Where's the nearest portal back to the human realm?"

She shot me a wide-eyed look. "I'm working on it, okay? Give me a minute." Closing her eyes, she lifted her head slightly as if trying to sense something. Her eyes snapped open and she let out a frustrated groan. "I don't know. I need time to work a proper spell. My power is too weak."

We couldn't just stand there waiting for her mojo to come back. We were too exposed in the clearing. In the distance, a rocky bluff rose above the trees. If we made for it, at least we might be able to hide among the rocks and remain undetected by whatever creatures lived in this part of Faerie.

"This way," I said, setting off into the forest.

Jim caught up with me. "I don't like this, Alec. Nothing good ever came from humans visiting the faerie realm."

"I know. Let's just hole up for a while and then get the hell out of Dodge when little miss sunshine decides she can find a portal."

He looked back at the rest of the group. "I'm worried about Frasier and Girard. Being chased by demons and ending up in Faerie isn't a good introduction to the preternatural world."

"Yeah," I said. "Girard seems to be taking it the worst, but Frasier might just be better at hiding it. We need to get them both back home as soon as we can."

"Yeah," Jim said. "This place might be pretty but it's too dangerous for humans."

He was right; Faerie was pretty. The quality of the light made everything seem vivid and colorful. As we strode through the forest, sparkling orbs danced between the trees, sometimes circling us in bright arcs. A light floral fragrance hung in the air and it smelled so good, I wanted to breathe it deep into my lungs and let the fragrance permeate my being.

But, as Jim had said, this beauty hid something dark and terrifying. There were cases throughout history of people being lost in the faerie realm, dragged here against their will, or tricked into becoming prisoners of the place's beauty.

Up ahead, the foot of the bluff came into view. The area was littered with huge boulders that looked as if they might have been thrown there by a giant.

Jim pointed to a dark cleft in the rock wall. "A cave."

I didn't much like the idea of entering a cave in this realm but the alternative was to stay out here in the open where we'd be seen by some passing denizen or other. If the cave wasn't too deep, we'd at least have a good defensive position and we'd only have to watch for danger coming from one direction.

When we arrived at the cave mouth, it was bigger than it had first looked, the crack reaching up at least thirty feet into the rock wall that formed the bluff above. The interior was gloomy for the first ten feet or so, and then was filled with impenetrable darkness.

I took out my Maglite and turned it on, playing the beam into the dark fissure. The dark tunnel stretched away, past the limit of my flashlight.

"What do you think?" Jim asked me.

"I think it looks more dangerous than a pit of vipers but if we stay close to the entrance, at least we'll be hidden from anyone or anything roaming the forest."

"Yeah, sounds good to me," he said.

We entered the cool, gloomy interior, followed by the others. "We'll take a break here," I told them, slipping my backpack off my shoulders and placing it on the ground. "We don't have any particular place to go anyway, until Gloria finds a portal that'll take us out of here."

Frasier and Girard sat down on the hard-packed dirt ground together and Gloria did likewise a few feet away from them, looking up at the high ceiling as if in thought.

Leon joined Jim and me and we went a little farther into the cave. The Maglite illuminated more tunnel running deeper into the ground. A cold chill swept over me and I was sure it wasn't only because the air was cooler back here. The hair on the back of my neck and my arms bristled

"Don't go back there," Gloria called. "It isn't safe."

I went over to her. "What do you mean? What do you know about this place?"

She frowned at me for a second and then a look of understanding passed over her face. "Oh, you don't know about the Shadow Land. Of course, how could you? That dreadful Society you're a part of thinks it knows everything but it hasn't even scratched the surface."

I sighed, already wishing we'd just kept walking through the forest. At least Gloria might have stayed quiet for a while. "What are you talking about?"

"The faerie realm is connected to the Shadow Land," she said. "You don't think horrible creatures like trolls and goblins come from the same place as me, do you?" She flashed me a smile.

"The Shadow Land," I prompted.

"The Shadow Land is the opposite of Faerie. Here, there is beauty, light, and eternal summer. The Shadow Land is a place of darkness, broken dreams and never-ending winter. Parts of it are actually formed from human nightmares. It's ugly and full of the dark faerie beings: trolls, goblins, hobgoblins, things like that." She wrinkled her nose in disgust.

"What does that have to do with this cave?" Jim asked her.

She looked fearfully at the shadows. "In places like this, the two realms meet. Dark places. Caves. Deep holes beneath the trees. The shadows beneath bridges. It's in these places that the dark beings can cross into Faerie."

"And vice versa," I said. "You could cross into the Shadow Land."

She wrinkled her nose again. "Why would anyone want to do that?"

"I'm just trying to get an understanding," I told her. "Like you said, the Society doesn't know about this. As far as I know, anyway."

"Where the realms touch, you could cross over either way," she said. "The Shadow Land touches your realm, as well. Places where bad things have happened in your realm are usually connected by a portal to the Shadow Land. The bad event creates the portal.

"When you humans have nightmares, you sometimes travel through the Shadow Land in your minds. The nightmare takes you to the places you fear. Some humans are more sensitive to it than others. I believe you call those people insane."

I looked at the darkness in the depths of the cave. Maybe we could go through there and find a way home, but from Gloria's description of the place, I'd rather find a portal in this realm. As much as I hated being in Faerie, it beat traveling through a land of nightmares.

"As soon as you can find a portal, do it," I told her.

"Yes, yes, all right," she said, turning away and folding her arms as if she were bored with me.

I went over to Frasier and Girard and sat with them. "How are you guys doing?"

"I think we're okay," Frasier said. The look of terror that had been in her eyes earlier was gone, replaced by a look of calm acceptance.

"I was just telling Claire about the time I thought I saw a Sasquatch," Girard said. "I was ten years old and me and my dad were fishing one of the lakes way out in the backcountry. He was a real old-fashioned type of guy, my dad, and was of the opinion that men should be men so he took me camping every year to teach me how to fish and hunt, and how to survive in the wilderness.

"This one time, we'd been at the lake a couple of days and my dad told me to go and catch something for supper while he chopped firewood. So I went down to the lake with my fishing rod and cast a few lures but nothing was biting. There was a creek maybe a half mile away and I decided I might have better luck there so I gathered up my tackle and went walking through the woods, hoping I'd get a couple of fish at the creek because if not, my dad was going to be mad.

"When I got near the creek, I heard some splashing and, thinking it might be fish jumping out of the water, I started running so I could see where they were feeding. But when I got to the water's edge, I froze. On the opposite bank there was a big, hairy creature that at first I thought was a black bear. It had the same kind of fur and it was kind of hunched over, dipping its paw into the water.

"But then it stood up and I could see it was no bear. It was like a person but taller than any person I'd ever seen. And it was covered in that black fur. It looked across the creek right at me and I was so scared, I peed myself. It looked at me for a couple of seconds and then it turned and disappeared into the trees. I turned tail and fled back to our campsite."

Girard took a deep breath and let it out slowly before continuing. "When I got back to the tent and told my dad what had happened, he told me I was stupid for making up a story like that and said I'd just been too lazy to catch our supper and was trying to get out of doing a bit of work. He laughed at me for wetting my pants. Then he went down to the lake and caught a fish for himself. But I wasn't allowed to have any. He told me if I couldn't be bothered to catch my own supper, then I could damned well go without. He said going hungry might teach me not to make up ridiculous stories."

He looked at me. "Do you think that was a real Sasquatch I saw? Over the years, I convinced myself that my eyes must have been playing tricks on me that day but now I'm not so sure."

"It sounds like you saw a Sasquatch," I told him. "They're shy creatures but there have been a few sightings."

Girard nodded slowly and looked down at the ground. He muttered to himself, "All my life, I thought my dad was right."

"Are we going to get out of here?" Frasier asked me.

"We're working on it," I told her, looking over at Gloria. The faerie queen was sitting with her eyes closed, hopefully building up her energy.

"I just keep thinking," Frasier said, "that if anything happens to me here, my husband and my kids will never know what happened to me. I'll have just disappeared from their lives. That isn't fair to them."

I put a comforting hand on her shoulder and looked into her eyes. "Listen to me. We're going to get out of here and you'll be back with your family soon. You trust Jim, don't you?"

She nodded.

"Well, he and I have been doing this kind of thing for a long time and we've been in worse predicaments than this. Don't worry, we'll get out of here."

"Okay," she said, "I believe you."

I gave her a reassuring smile and went over to Gloria. "How's it going?"

She opened her eyes and let out a sigh. "My power is returning slowly. I need my torc. I can't go on much longer like this. This must be what it feels like to be human."

"Where is the torc, anyway?" I asked her.

"Hidden."

"Yeah, I know that, but since you're taking us to the place where it's hidden, you might as well tell me where it is."

She thought about it for a moment and then said, "I suppose so. If it were anyone else asking me the question, I might refuse, but I've watched you, Alec Harbinger. You're a plain-speaking, honest man. You wouldn't betray me and take the torc for yourself."

"No, I wouldn't," I said truthfully.

"The torc has been hidden in many places over time," she said, "but the last place I hid it was in England."

"England? So what are doing here in Canada?"

"I told you, my escape routes were limited. And at the time I hid the portal, there was no Canada or America."

"You hid it a long time ago?"

"Yes, a long time ago in your human reckoning, she said. "It was a time when the people of that land and the people of my realm, the faeries, were quite close. They communed with us frequently and wrote stories and songs and poems about us. The land was mostly forest save for a few towns and villages and my people--who frolicked among the trees and springs--were seen as guardians of the wilderness by the people who lived in those places.

"It was during this time that I gave the torc to my sister Vivian, the Lady of the Lake. She doesn't live in Faerie—she's bound to your realm—and her task is to guard items of power. So she was the perfect choice to guard my torc."

"Okay," I said, "so where is your sister?"

"She resides in a lake on Bodmin Moor. Are you familiar with Cornwall?"

"Not really," I admitted.

"A lovely place. There are kings and queens and knights and everyone believes in magic and the faerie people."

I arched a skeptical eyebrow at her. "It sounds like you're talking about the Middle Ages. Do you really think the torc will still be where you left it?"

"I told you, it's protected by my sister! I wish I hadn't said anything now. I tell you the truth, yet you still question me."

I held up my hands in an effort to placate her. "Hey, I was only asking a question. If you don't want to talk about it, fine. I'll leave you alone for a while so you can build up enough power to get us out of here. As I walked away, I added, "And get over yourself."

"Alec, wait, I'm sorry," Gloria said in a whiny tone. "Come back, please."

I went back over to her and said, "Are you going to play nice now?"

But she was ignoring me, looking over at the cave mouth and the forest beyond. When she turned her face back to me, I saw the wide, terrified look in her eyes. "They're here," she said. "They found us."

CHAPTER 18

Felicity was worry-stricken. She hadn't heard from Alec for three days now and she was sure something was very wrong. She'd left dozens of messages and sent him twice as many texts but he'd gone silent.

She'd even tried ringing the office phone on the off-chance that he might be there but that had just rung and then gone to the answering machine.

Now, as she paced her parents' patio, unable to sit still because of the nervous energy she felt, she wondered if she should get a flight back to Maine. If Alec was in some sort of trouble and turned up in Dearmont, he might need her and she'd be no good to him here in England.

She looked out over the countryside. Evening was approaching, darkening the surrounding fields and trees and turning the sky a dull red. In the distance, a flock of starlings appeared as a black, swirling cloud and cried out as they found their roost for the night.

Felicity's phone rang and she grabbed it from her jeans pocket and inspected the screen. The number it displayed was unknown to her. "Hello?"

The man on the other end of the line had a slight German accent. "Miss Lake, this is Hans Lieben from the Society. I'm calling about Alec Harbinger."

She didn't want to tell this man—a total stranger—that Alec was missing, so she kept her cool and simply said, "Yes?"

"Do you know where he is, Miss Lake? I have received a message that he wishes me to call him but I cannot reach him."

"No, I'm not sure," Felicity said. She didn't know if she could confide in this man or not. He said he was from the Society but she had no proof of that. And the Society still had Midnight Cabal spies within its ranks so even if Hans Lieben was telling the truth, it didn't mean Felicity should trust him.

There was a pause on the other end of the line and then Lieben said, "It is very important that I speak with Alec as soon as possible. Could you please ask him to contact me as a matter of urgency?"

"I thought you said he left a message for *you* to call *him*," Felicity said.

"That is true, yes. He wished to speak to me regarding his father. I have information on the matter that I wish to talk to Alec about."

"What is it?" Felicity asked, her curiosity piqued. "I'm not sure when Alec will be able to get back to you but you can tell me the information, if you like, and I'll pass it on to him."

There was another pause and then Lieben said, "Very well, I will speak to you, Miss Lake, but not like this, not over the phone. Perhaps we can meet somewhere?"

Alarm bells went off in Felicity's head. She had no idea who this man was and meeting him could be dangerous. But, on the other hand, it wasn't as if she had anything that Lieben wanted; she had no idea where Alec was any more than he did. So even if Lieben was working for the bad guys, Felicity couldn't let slip any information that could put Alec in danger.

And what if Lieben was one of the good guys? Felicity owed it to Alec to get whatever information she could out of Lieben since Alec wasn't here to do it himself.

"All right," she said, "I'll meet you. But where? Are you in London?"

"Not at the moment. I'm currently in Plymouth. You are quite close by, I believe, in Sussex."

"How did you..?" She was going to ask him how he knew where she was but then remembered that there were many ways the Society could track her. Unlike Alec, she didn't have tattoos that protected her from location spells or scrying. "Never mind," she said, "where would you like to meet?"

"I can get my driver to bring me to you," he suggested.

Felicity decided that whether Hans Lieben was a good guy or not, she didn't want him coming to her parents' house. She wanted to choose the location of the meeting herself and make sure it was in a crowded, public place. "That isn't really convenient," she said, "and I don't want to drive all the way to Plymouth so perhaps we could meet somewhere in the middle? How about Exeter? There's a coffee shop there called Fresh Grounds. Do you know it?" She'd been there a few times with her mother. Even though the city was a three-hour drive away, they'd made that drive on numerous occasions to visit Exeter's gothic cathedral and spend the rest of the day shopping.

"No," Lieben said, "but I'm sure I can find it."

"Tomorrow then," she said. "Shall we say one-thirty?" That would give her plenty of time to make the drive.

"Very well, Miss Lake. I shall see you then." He hung up.

Felicity put her phone away and went into the house. Her parents were in the living room watching *Midsomer Murders* and didn't notice her go up to her room. She decided not to disturb them. She'd tell them in the morning that she was going to Exeter.

When she got to her room, she lay on the bed and tried Alec's number again but her call went straight to voicemail as usual.

Alec," she whispered into the darkness, "where are you?"

CHAPTER 19

I TOLD THE OTHERS TO prepare for an attack and hefted my backpack over my shoulders in case we needed to make a quick exit. When the pack was situated firmly on my back, I drew my sword. Jim, Leon, and Girard had done the same. The blue glow from the blades lit up the cave. Frasier was crouched in a firing stance, her gun pointed at the forest.

"What is it?" I asked Gloria. "What's coming?"

"The name is Davos," came a cold voice from the shadows beneath the trees. A tall, thin man dressed in a dark suit and red tie stepped forward slightly. He had long, straight, black hair that reached down below his shoulders. When he reached the edge of the shadows, he stopped. "The sunlight in this realm doesn't affect me quite so adversely as that in our own but I prefer to remain here if that's all right with you."

"That's fine with me," I said. "You can stay there all day for all I care."

He flashed me a predatory grin. "Now, Mr. Harbinger, is that any way to greet a new acquaintance? And all of these weapons that you and your friends are brandishing are quite unnecessary."

"You're no acquaintance of mine," I told him. "I know who you work for."

"I don't work for anyone," he corrected me. "I work *with* the Midnight Cabal. Working with them suits my needs, that is all. Now, speaking of working with people, perhaps you'd like to work with me and hand over the faerie." He pointed a long finger at Gloria, who shrank back against the cave wall, fear written in her face and posture.

"I can't do that," I told Davos. "I'm sworn to protect her."

He chuckled. It was a dry, rustling sound, like dead leaves falling onto a grave. "And I thought chivalry died long ago. You're a Society-man through and through, Alec Harbinger. You must have inherited that from your father."

"Leave my father out of this. You came here for the faerie queen, and I'm telling you I'm sworn to protect her. So either leave or make your move." Even as I said the words, I realized I was calling out an ancient vampire. Not a wise move. But I refused to show fear to this creature.

Davos looked amused. "You certainly have spirit, Alec. But I tire of this conversation. We both know I can take the faerie whenever I want to. I'm simply trying to avoid bloodshed."

"A vampire trying to avoid bloodshed," I said. "That's the first time I've heard that one."

"Don't be so cynical," he said. "I have reasons for not wanting to spill your blood but I will do so if there is no alternative."

"You're all heart," I said. But my bravado was hiding something else: fear for my friends. They'd been drawn into this because of my bargain with Gloria and because of that, I felt responsible for their lives. As far as I could see, there was only one way for us to get out of here and that was through the dark tunnel at the rear of the cave, into the Shadow Land.

That might put us in even more danger but facing an ancient vampire here and now, without the proper weapons or equipment, was a death sentence.

Besides, maybe the Shadow Land wasn't all that bad. Gloria was terrified of the place but she had a tendency to over-dramatize everything.

I said to the others, "I'll hold him off for as long as I can while you guys make a run for it. Get to the tunnel."

"No," Gloria said, "I can't go in there. Don't make me."

"You either go in there or you face the vampire," I told her.

Her eyes turned reluctantly to the darkness at the back of the cave, then back to me, and I wondered if she might actually be considering staying here and facing Davos.

But Jim took her arm and led her back there. Frasier and Girard followed.

Leon hesitated. "Are you coming too, man?"

"Yeah, I'll be there in a minute," I said. "Now, go."

He went.

Leaving me to face the ancient vampire alone.

"Alec," Davos said, "how long do you think you can you keep running? Do you really think you and your ragtag group of friends have any hope against the Midnight Cabal? The reason Korax, Damalis, and I are working with them is because they're going to win this war and become the most powerful organization in the world. Your Society of Shadows will be nothing more than dust in the dark wind. You can't fight us. You're nothing more than a minor annoyance, a bug to be swatted away and then forgotten."

"I'd rather be a minor annoyance than no annoyance at all," I told him.

He smiled coldly. "That's the trouble with people like you; you don't dream big. You content yourself with a pathetic, short life and tell yourself that you're making a difference somehow, making other people's pathetic, short lives better. Your altruism sickens me. Why not take life by the throat and throttle every last gasp out of it for yourself?"

"And be like you?" I asked. "Work for the Midnight Cabal and try to put humanity back into a state of superstition and fear?"

"Yes, make them fear us. Do you know what it's like to be feared? Do you know how powerful it makes you?"

"You're nothing but a group of bullies," I said. "You have an inflated sense of self-importance and need to force others to fear you to make yourselves feel good. And you say *my* life is pathetic?" I forced a laugh of disdain out of my throat, hoping my stalling had given the others enough time to cross over into the Shadow Land, because I was getting ready to make a run for it myself.

Davos wasn't affected by my insults—I was sure he'd heard much worse in three-and-a-half thousand years of existence—but it felt good to tell him what I really thought of him and the organization he worked for.

He grinned. "Alec, you stand there insulting things of which you have no comprehension and yet the most insulting thing is that you think I don't know what you're doing. There is only one reason a fly speaks to a spider and that is to delay the inevitable. You believe that even as we stand here conversing, your friends are escaping into the Shadow Land." He laughed. It was a thin sound like a cold breeze blowing across a graveyard. "You are mistaken."

I heard a noise behind me and turned to see Gloria, Jim, Frasier, and Girard being led out of the shadows by demons, their hands restrained behind their backs. Their weapons were in the arms of one of the demons.

When I turned back to face Davos, he was suddenly standing right in front of me. I stepped back reflexively, swinging the sword at him, not really aiming at any part of him in particular, just taking a wild swing.

He side-stepped the blade and moved forward so fast I wasn't aware of his attack until I felt his cold hand around my throat. He looked into my eyes with a malevolent glare. I looked away, not because I was afraid of him but because I couldn't let him glamor me.

Davos lifted me off the ground with one hand and took my sword from me with the other. As my weapon clattered to the ground, I fought against the vampire with my arms and legs, kicking at him and struggling in his grasp, grabbing his hand with my own and trying to tear it from my throat so I could breathe, but he was too strong and my efforts were wasted.

His mouth curled into a snarl. "After existing for millennia, few things give me pleasure anymore. Killing you might give me some satisfaction but it would be brief and soon would be no more than a pleasant memory. But I know the type of man you are, Alec, and I know making you live with the knowledge that you failed to protect someone is a far worse punishment than merely killing you."

He threw me into the shadows and, as the cold blackness enveloped me, I heard Davos say, "Enjoy your nightmares."

CHAPTER 20

BLACKNESS TOTALLY ENGULFED ME FOR a second and then I landed on my back in a dark forest. I scrambled to my feet and looked around.

Behind me, there was a sheer rock face and a dark tunnel that I'd just been thrown from, the tunnel between here and Faerie. I ran back into it, not sure what I hoped to achieve with no weapons, but unwilling to leave my friends in the clutches of Davos and his demons.

But the tunnel only went so far before terminating in a natural stone wall. There was no portal back to Faerie. After throwing me through, Davos had sealed it somehow.

I stalked out of the cave and into the trees, suddenly aware of how cold it was here. Gloria had said the Shadow Land was a place of never-ending winter and it looked like she was right about that. Where orbs of light floated in the

Faerie forest, here there were flakes of snow drifting on a cold wind. The sky was a deep, gloomy blue that was shot through with gray snow-clouds.

An urgent, whispered voice came from the trees. "Alec!"

I looked in the direction of the sound and saw Leon coming toward me. He seemed relieved to see me. "I thought I was here alone," he said. "When the demons attacked, I got separated from the others." He looked around. "Where is everybody?"

"The demons caught them and took them back to Faerie," I told him. "Davos sealed the way back. We're going to have to find another way out of here."

"I hear that," Leon said, shooting a nervous glance at the forest around us. "And the sooner the better. This place gives me the creeps."

"Me too," I agreed. "Gloria said it was a place of nightmares and it definitely has a nightmarish quality about it. Let's just hope we don't run into the boogeyman. We don't have any weapons."

"Yeah, I lost my sword somewhere," Leon said.

"The demons will have picked it up," I told him. "No point worrying about it now. Let's find a way out of here."

He nodded. "Any idea which direction we should try?"

"I don't think it matters. From what Gloria said, I don't think the usual laws of time and space apply here. Parts of this realm are formed from nightmares so the place is probably fluid, like thought. There might not be any static locations."

He looked at me dubiously. "Then how do we find a portal if their locations keep changing?"

"I don't know," I admitted. "Let's just go this way and try to get a better vantage point so we can see what's around us. These trees can't go on forever." I pointed at the forest directly ahead of us and we went in that direction. In a world where there might not be any true directions, this one was as good as any.

"It's cold," Leon said after a few minutes of trudging through the undergrowth.

"Yeah," I agreed.

We went a little farther in silence and then he asked, "What's the plan now? We going to rescue the others?"

"Yeah, we are. But first, we're going to get that torc. Before those vampires force Gloria to tell them its location, we're going to steal it out from under their noses. Then we're going to carry out a rescue mission and give it to Gloria so she can regain her powers and take back her part of Faerie."

"You make it sound so simple, man. I'm in."

I gave him a grim smile. "But first, we need to get out of this place."

"Not so simple," he said.

"No."

He began to say something else but stopped, listened, and then said, "Do you hear that?"

178

I listened to the forest around us. All I could hear was the snow falling on the leaves above us. "No, what is it?"

"Not in the trees," he said. "Closer. Like it's under the ground at our feet."

I felt it then, a digging sound beneath the earth, accompanied now by a vibration that shuddered through the ground.

"What the hell is that?" My question was answered as the ground beneath me burst open and a pair of clawed hands reached up and grabbed my legs.

I was pulled downward by strong arms and the last thing I saw before I was dragged into the ground was Leon being similarly taken. He looked at me with wide, terror-stricken eyes, his hands clawing at the earth in front of his face, before he disappeared into the ground.

Then my vision became dark and the smell of earth, tree roots, and something foul like putrid flesh filled my nostrils. I was dimly aware of the claws dragging me through a tunnel but I couldn't fight back.

Maybe the claws had injected me with some sort of poison or maybe the stench down here was a gas that affected my nervous system, but whichever was the case, I was totally paralyzed. I could only allow myself to be dragged along the subterranean tunnel, hoping that whatever was keeping me immobile would wear off eventually.

The tunnel widened into a chamber where I was lifted to my feet and slammed against a wall. Thick tree roots were pulled around me, trapping me in place. Across the small chamber, I could see Leon likewise trapped. There was light here, provided by a dimly-glowing crystal set in the earth at the center of the chamber. In its dull glow, I could see our captors.

There were two of them. They were the size of humans but were covered in ragged black fur. Their heads were featureless ovals of gray, like huge membranous sacks. They had huge claws that were obviously perfect for digging.

One of them went over to Leon and placed its hand on the side of his head. Leon seemed to fall into a deep sleep. Veins within the creature's head began to pulse.

The second creature came over to me and reached for my head. I felt the cold touch of its hand and then the chamber faded from my sight.

* * *

I became aware of the smell of gas and then my vision returned and I was sitting in the back seat of my mother's car. It was nighttime. The windshield was shot through with a web of cracks, there was white smoke rising into the air beyond the side windows and we were at the side of the road, on the shoulder.

I knew this moment of my life; it was the moment my mom was killed. Only now, I wasn't just remembering it, I was sitting next to my younger self in the back seat of the car, as if in a dream.

The younger version of me was panicked, his eyes wide.

My mom turned in her seat, her face full of concern, and said to him, "Alec, are you okay?"

"Yeah, I think so," he said. His voice sounded young, higher-pitched than mine was today.

"Listen closely," she told him. "You need to get out of the car and run. You see those woods over there?"

I wanted to tell her no. I was here now, the older version of myself. I could protect her from whatever was coming to get her. I said, "No, Mom, I can help you now."

She didn't hear me, of course.

The younger me looked out of the windows at the trees barely visible through the smoke and said, "Yeah, I see them."

"I want you to go ahead and open your door and run into the woods, okay?" She cast a nervous glance at the rearview mirror.

I could hear footsteps behind the car. They approached slowly, carefully.

I turned in the seat to look out of the rear window but there was nothing there but a gray fog. It was as if I could only see what I'd seen when I'd actually been here all those years ago. I couldn't remember something I'd never seen.

"Alec, go," my mom said. "And whatever happens, don't look back, okay?"

"But, Mom…"

"Please, Alec. Run for the trees. And don't stop running."

My younger self unfastened his seatbelt and opened the car door.

I shouted at him, "No, stay here! If you stay here, I can stay here too and help Mom!"

The smell of gas and burning rubber drifted into the car, making my eyes water even though I knew I wasn't really here. This was a vision into the past and no matter how much I wanted to change the events unfolding before my eyes, I couldn't.

My mom's eyes were watering too when she reached back to touch my younger self's arm and said, "I love you, Alec. No matter what happens in your life, always remember that I loved you."

He hesitated, unsure what to say.

"Tell her you love her too!" I shouted at him.

But he was just a confused kid and didn't realize that he was about to lose his mother forever.

"Now, go," Mom whispered to him. "Hurry." He slid out of the car and ran for the trees and suddenly I was out of the car too, following after him despite my desire to stay and fight.

Younger Me glanced over his shoulder and I knew it was because he was expecting to see Mom following him to safety. But she wasn't there.

I looked back too and saw four dark figures walking calmly up to the burning, crumpled car. Then a flash of intense blue light shot from the vehicle and one of the figures fell to the ground. The other three hesitated for a moment before rushing the car.

"Run, Alec!" Mom shouted.

Young Alec ran and I followed. Behind us, flashes of light of various colors illuminated the sky as if someone were igniting fireworks.

We ran into the woods, branches and pine needles whipping at us. I felt the pain of losing my mother all over again and even though I knew this was just a dream, that didn't dull my emotions. I cursed my younger self for running. It would have been cathartic to save her, even if this was only a scene playing inside my head.

That thought brought me to my senses. I'd been so lost inside the dream that I hadn't been concerned about the fact that I was trapped in an underground chamber in the Shadow Land while a creature had its hand on my head.

Was it making me relive this moment? Could it see what I was seeing or was it just feeding off my raw emotions?

Younger Alec had stopped running and was sitting beneath a tall pine, crying. This was the moment his life was about to change. After his mother's death in a supposed car accident, his father would come to London and take him to study in the Academy of Shadows where he'd learn to be an investigator.

And just a couple of weeks from this moment, his father would take him to the Coven, the witches that ran the Society of Shadows, and have them cast an enchantment on the boy that would inscribe magical symbols on his bones.

As I stood over my younger, crying self, that gave me pause for thought. I wasn't really here. I was in that subterranean chamber being fed on by a creature. I had no weapons, but maybe I could use my magic to break out.

Into my mind, I summoned the magical circle that symbolized the energy blast and I concentrated on it. It burned bright blue in my mind's eye and I felt a heat rising within me. I kept it in check until it had increased in intensity so much that I could hear it humming in my ears. Then I released its power in a blast that exploded out from me in all directions.

* * *

Suddenly, I wasn't in the dream anymore. I was standing in the subterranean chamber surrounded by broken roots. I was free. The creature that had been feeding from me was lying on the ground. It wasn't moving but I had no way of knowing if it was dead or not. The damned thing didn't even have any eyes.

The creature that had been feeding on Leon turned in surprise, its hand leaving his head. I kicked it with the sole of my boot, slamming it into the wall of the chamber. It made a chittering sound and lunged at me, swiping the air with its claws. I dodged the attack and used its own momentum to send it sprawling onto the ground.

There was nothing handy that I could use as a weapon so I slid the backpack from my shoulders and swung it by its straps at the membranous head. The head exploded, covering my arms in a gray, viscous fluid. I stepped back, instinctively trying to wipe the stuff off me, expecting that it might be acidic or poisonous, but it seemed harmless.

"Eeew, that's gross, man," Leon said. He was still trapped by the roots but very much awake now.

I pulled at the roots, loosening them and helping him break free. "Let's get the hell out of here before any more of these things show up."

"You don't have to tell me twice. That dude gave me a god-awful nightmare."

"Me too. I think they were feeding on our emotions."

We followed the tunnel back to the holes we'd been dragged down, and climbed out.

Leon looked at the trees around us. "Now we wander aimlessly again until some other monster shows up to kill us."

"Yeah, I'm getting pissed-off too," I said. "There has to be a way of finding those portals. There should be plenty of them around because this realm touches our own in so many places. Gloria said the crossover points are where bad things have happened in our world."

"But we're not in our world, we're in this one. It isn't like we can go to the Lizzie Borden house and find the portal to the Shadow Land. We're already in the Shadow Land, on this side of the portal. We don't know where the Lizzie Borden house is on this side."

"Wait a minute," I said, "you have a point. If there's a portal in the bad places, then there must be a Shadow Land version of those places. So we just have to find one."

"Yeah, well, I have a newsflash for you: this place isn't laid out like our world. You said time and space are different here."

I was thinking now, getting an idea. "They are. Gloria said that when we have nightmares, we travel across this land in our minds. Except we can't do that because we're actually, physically here. But if our thoughts can transport us across the Shadow Land…"

"We can think ourselves out of here!" Leon said.

"Not exactly. But we may be able to get to a place where there's a portal."

He nodded. "I get it. So, if we think of the Lizzie Borden house, we'll arrive at the Shadow Land version of it. Then we find the portal to our own realm and go through it into the real Lizzie Borden house in our world."

"Yeah, but maybe not the Lizzie Borden house. That's a bed- and-breakfast now in our world so we wouldn't want to suddenly appear there. It might take some explaining. We need somewhere that's abandoned."

He thought for a moment and then suggested, "*The Amityville Horror* house?"

"No, someone owns that now. It's a family home. I've got it: Blackthorn House, the place where the Bloody Summer Night Massacre took place. A lot of bad things happened there so it has to have a Shadow Land version. Also, I can picture it in my mind. I've never been there but I've seen photos of the place."

"Yeah, me too. That's where Mallory was almost killed, right? By that Mister Scary dude."

"Yeah, that's the place. She's told me about it so many times, I've had nightmares of that house myself." I didn't add that I'd also had a nightmare about a house I'd never even heard of, the mysterious house numbered 19 where I'd dreamed about Mallory in a mirror.

Leon nodded slowly, pity in his eyes. "She's a great girl. It's a shame she had to put up with all that shit."

"Agreed. Now, picture the house in your mind. Imagine you're standing right outside it." Leon closed his eyes. I did the same and imagined I was standing before the house where the Bloody Summer Night Massacre had happened, where Mallory had emerged as the sole survivor, the Final Girl.

When I opened my eyes, I was still standing in the forest next to Leon.

"Shit," he said. "So that isn't how it works."

I sighed, frustrated. "Obviously not." Then the weakness came over me and I leaned against a tree, trying to stay upright. But the strength in my arms and legs faded and I slid down the trunk until I was sitting on the ground.

"You okay?' Leon asked, putting a hand on my shoulder to keep me from falling to one side.

"I will be in a minute. I used an energy blast to get out of that induced dream."

"Just take it easy," he said.

The image of the bright red magical circle with the unicursal hexagram came into my head. I ignored it, choosing to wait out the weakness and recover my strength slowly. Leon was the only living being in the vicinity as far as I knew, and I didn't want my magic to drain his life force. I concentrated instead on the trunk of the tree in front of me and eventually, the red magical symbol faded.

And so did my consciousness. The world around me faded as I blacked out. Images flashed through my mind, images of Blackthorn House and the horror that had occurred there. Malory had told me some of the gory details about the night Mister Scary decided to visit the high school party in the abandoned house and my mind played over those details before the images gradually faded away and I regained consciousness.

"Alec," Leon said, his voice worried. "Are you awake, man?"

"Yeah," I said groggily. "Sorry, I kind of shut down for a second there." I looked up at him. He was looking at something behind me with wide eyes.

"What's wrong?" I asked.

"We aren't in the forest anymore."

I looked past him, where a moment ago there had been trees. Instead, there was a street with houses on either side of the road. It was nighttime and there was still snow falling but the forest was gone. A gray fog hung in the air, giving the place an eerie atmosphere. The houses were mainly large mansion-type buildings but their details were difficult to discern because there was a shadowy quality about them, as if they were a dim reflection of actual places.

Most of them were set back away from the road behind iron fences and overgrown grounds. Leon and I were behind one of those fences ourselves and I realized I wasn't leaning on a tree anymore; my back was pressed against a set of porch steps.

Struggling to my feet, I turned and saw the large clapboard house whose grounds we stood on. Blackthorn House. The site of the Bloody Summer Massacre. I'd only ever seen it on TV but it was unmistakable with its Victorian design that included an assortment of second-floor balconies and a turret in the western corner.

Leon said, "One second we were in the forest, the next, we were here."

"Let's hope there's a portal to the Blackthorn House in our world inside," I said.

"You feeling up to taking a look?" he asked me.

"Yeah, I'm fine." My strength was returning slowly and I felt strong enough to move, even if I wasn't exactly in fighting condition. "Let's go," I said, ascending the creaky wooden steps to the porch.

The house had double front doors, carved with leaves and vines and gargoyle heads.

"This place is creepy as fuck," Leon said. "Why the hell did those kids decide to have a party here?"

"The creepiness probably added to the excitement. Kids that age feel invincible, like nothing can hurt them. I guess they learned the hard way that there are real horrors in the world."

I pushed the double doors and they opened, revealing a dark hallway and stair leading to the upper floors. I turned on my Maglite and shone the beam inside.

There were dead bodies in there, or at least the shadowy reflections of dead bodies. They lay on the floor in various death poses but there was something unsubstantial about them. Their features were blurry and I could see the floor beneath them, as if they were made of wispy black smoke.

"What the hell?" Leon said as the flashlight beam played over the smoky corpses.

"This Shadow Land version of the house seems to be locked in time at the moment of the massacre," I said.

Leon looked at me, concerned. "Do you think Mister Scary is here?"

I listened to the quiet of Blackthorn House, wondering if Mister Scary was in there somewhere, hiding and waiting for us to enter. "I don't think so," I said. "He's moved on since the massacre that took place in this house. I don't see why he'd be here."

"Unless he enjoys revisiting the scene of the crime," Leon pointed out. He pointed at the street and the other houses. "Do you think these are all his crime scenes? Like, his own corner of Shadow Land?"

I followed his gaze to the houses on either side of the road. There were at least a dozen. Had Mister Scary been that prolific? Maybe there were murders that hadn't been attributed to him, earlier crimes that he'd committed while evolving into the killer who would eventually carry out the Bloody Summer Night Massacre.

"They could be," I said to Leon.

He turned his attention back to the darkness within Blackthorn House and swallowed. "Okay, so where are we going to look for this portal?"

"I don't know. I don't even know what it is we're looking for. The portals between our world and Faerie are usually circles of stones or flowers but the portals to and from the Shadow Land could be something entirely different." I remembered my dream of Mallory. "Maybe it's mirrors. This realm is a reflection of our own, so maybe mirrors are the portals." I stepped into the house.

"So let's find a mirror," Leon said, following me.

"I remember seeing some photos of the house when the massacre hit the news," I said. "There was a full-length mirror in one of the bedrooms." I went to the foot of the stairs and shone my light up to the second floor. "I'm guessing it's somewhere up there."

The beam of the Maglite showed peeling wallpaper with a rose design and more smoky shadows of dead bodies on the stairs.

We went up, stepping over the bodies even though they were no more than smoke. At the top of the stairs, a corridor led to the left and right. There were doors in each direction—some closed, some open—and another staircase leading up to the next floor.

"Let's check this floor first," I suggested. "If we don't find what we're looking for, we'll go up to the next level." I turned right and went to the first open door. It opened onto a bedroom, although the bed and other furniture were insubstantial shadows like the bodies on the floor. There was no mirror.

"It's here," Leon said from behind me. He was looking through the door on the opposite side of the corridor. "There's a mirror."

I turned and went into the room. The large window looked out at the street and let in a dim glow of moonlight. On the wall was a full-length mirror. Unlike everything else we'd seen in the house, the mirror was real. The Maglite beam reflected off the glass.

"Look," Leon said, pointing to a red smear in the top right corner.

I moved closer and inspected it. "It's a bloody handprint."

"You think one of the murdered kids touched the mirror before they died?"

"No, it's in this side, in the Shadow Land. The victims aren't much more than shadows here. They wouldn't leave a handprint like this. It's as real as the mirror it's on."

"So someone else put it there."

I considered this new development. From what Gloria had said, it sounded as if bad places in our realm cast a shadow into the Shadow Land *after* the bad thing had happened at that location. So I wouldn't have thought this shadow version of Blackthorn House would exist until after the Bloody Summer Night Massacre.

But what if I was looking at it the wrong way, at least as far as Mister Scary was concerned? What if he'd created the shadow version in this realm and used it to get into the real version of the house? It would explain how he disappeared after Mallory shot him and it would account for him seemingly appearing out of nowhere on the night of the murder.

The police had theorized that he must have already been hiding in the house when the kids had shown up for the party but what if he'd used this mirror to step from the Shadow Land version of the house into the real one?

But how could he have created a Shadow Land version before the night of the massacre?

"He's dreaming the murders," I said.

"What?" Leon had been examining the mirror. Now, he looked at me with questioning eyes.

"Mister Scary. He dreams about the murders before he carries them out. Gloria said parts of the Shadow Land are formed by dreams or nightmares, so his dreams create the shadow versions of the houses. Then he uses the portals in the shadow versions to get into the actual houses and commit the murders he's been dreaming about."

Leon thought about it. "That's why the police never catch him at the scene of the crime. He comes back here, into the shadow version, and escapes."

"Yeah, this explains it." I pointed at the mirror. "If there's more than one mirror in the house, it might even explain how he moves from room to room unseen."

"What about the bloody handprint?"

"I assume that's how the portal is charged. Most magical portals require some kind of sacrifice to activate them and shedding your own blood is one of the most powerful sacrifices of all."

"So all we have to do is cut ourselves, touch the mirror, and we're out of here?"

I nodded. "It probably is that simple."

He fished a pocket knife out of his jeans. "You want to go first?"

"Wait," I said, "we need to think about this. If we rush through this portal, we might be missing an opportunity to get even closer to the torc."

"Are you sure we can't just leave?' Leon said, moving to the window and looking out at the street below. "I don't want to hang around here a second longer than I have to."

"Blackthorn House is in New York State," I told him. "If we go through the portal and end up there, we'll still need to get to England where the torc is hidden. Maybe we could find a portal in this realm that takes us to England."

"You mean think of a bad place in England like we did to get here?"

I nodded. "It'll save us time, something we don't have a lot of if we're going to beat the vampires to the torc."

Leon nodded, still looking out of the window. "Okay, but I don't know of any creepy houses in England where murders took place."

I racked my brain. I wasn't sure I knew of any either. I'd spent years in London while I was studying at the Academy of Shadows but I hadn't exactly sought out murder houses. There were countless "Ripper Tours" in the city that visited the places where Jack the Ripper had committed his crimes but I'd never been on any of them. I tried to remember the other places I'd visited and if any of them cold be described as a "bad place."

"The only place I can think of is the Tower of London," I told Leon. "Two young princes were murdered there in the fifteenth century but I don't know if that's enough to create a portal to the Shadow Land, or if it was so long ago that the shadow version of the tower might have faded away."

"Alec, we don't have time for this," Leon said. "We've got company."

I went to the window and looked down at the street. At the end of the street, in the fog, stood a man. He was in silhouette and I couldn't make out any details of his face but I could see that he held an ax. The hairs on the back of my neck stood up. When the man turned his face to the window where we stood, Leon and I instinctively took a step back.

"Is that him?" Leon whispered.

"Yeah, I think so." My own voice had also dropped to whisper. "We need to get out of here. Now."

We went to the mirror quickly and Leon handed me his pocket knife.

I took it from him and opened the blade before drawing it across my palm. When the cut turned bright red with blood, I placed my hand on the mirror.

The activation of the portal manifested itself as a slight darkening of the reflection. I reached forward with my hand and, instead of meeting the glass, my fingers went through, disappearing into the mirror.

I stepped forward and found myself in a room just like the one in the Shadow Land except there daylight beyond the window and the furniture here was the real thing and not a smoky shadow.

Leon stepped into the room and the reflection in the mirror behind him became normal.

He went to the window and looked out. "I think we're home."

"Yeah. Well, we're in New York State, anyway. Not too far from home. We can get a flight back to Maine. Then we need to get to England and find that torc."

"Without passports?" Leon asked. "I don't know about you but I left mine in my luggage at Jim's house."

"I think I know a way around that. We can get back to Maine using our drivers licenses and then I'll sort out the passport situation. We just have to hope we get to the torc before Gloria cracks. I'd imagine that after three thousand years, those vampires know some effective ways of getting information out of someone."

"And I don't think Gloria is going to keep her mouth shut for long," Leon said as we left the bedroom and descended the stairs.

"You never know," I said, "she might be more resilient than we think. She's a faerie queen, after all. Sure, she's ditzy when she's playing a human but maybe she has an inner strength we haven't seen yet."

"I sure hope so."

The double doors that led outside were locked so we found a window in the living room and went out that way. When we finally stood beneath the sun in the grounds of the house, I took in a deep breath of air, glad to be home.

The sight of Mister Scary had unnerved me in such a way that I felt it even more important to reach Mallory and stop her going after him alone. He was more than just a man; he seemed to have the ability to manipulate the Shadow Land to help him carry out his murders. Mallory was underestimating him, believing him to be nothing more than a regular psychopathic killer, and that was dangerous.

"Let's never go back there again," Leon said.

I nodded in agreement. If it were up to me, I'd never go to Faerie again either but I knew that once we had the torc, we were going to have to go back and rescue our friends.

And this time, we would be armed with weapons to destroy vampires. I didn't take kindly to having my friends taken.

Ancient vampire or not, I was ready to make Davos pay.

CHAPTER 21

Felicity sat in the Fresh Grounds coffee shop waiting for Hans Lieben to appear. She'd been here an hour already, having left her parents house immediately after breakfast. Her father had been happy enough to lend her the Volvo and had seemed glad that Felicity was taking some time away from the house. The drive to Exeter had gone smoothly and she'd arrived with time to spare. After finding a parking space, she'd decided to go straight to the coffee shop and wait.

Now, it was time for Lieben to put in an appearance and Felicity felt a growing anxiety. Was she making the right decision by coming here? Was Lieben really who he said he was or was he a member of the Midnight Cabal posing as a Society member? Yesterday, his phone call had taken Felicity off guard and she had agreed to this meeting perhaps a little too hastily. Now, she felt anxious and wary and wondered if she should have come here at all.

On the table in front of her sat her third latte. It was untouched because Felicity didn't think that more caffeine would be good for her already-frayed nerves. A couple of times, she'd been tempted to leave the coffee shop and not look back but if Lieben was genuine and had some information that was important to Alec, she would never forgive herself if she missed out on it just because of her paranoia.

Flesh Grounds was bustling with patrons. Judging by the amount of suits and smart attire, most were here to grab a coffee during their lunch break before returning to work. At a table near the door, five smartly-dressed women were holding some sort of meeting, their table covered with papers containing graphs and figures. The air was filled with the sound of chatter and the hiss of the coffee machine.

Felicity had chosen a table near the window that looked out on the busy street. Through the slightly-misted glass, she saw a tall, thin man in a tan raincoat approach the shop. He had close-cropped blonde hair and wore wire-rimmed glasses. Under one arm, he carried a newspaper. When he entered Fresh Grounds, Felicity was sure he was Hans Lieben.

He saw her and gave her a slight wave, as if he knew her. *Of course he knows me*, Felicity thought. *He's probably seen my picture in the Society's personnel records.*

While Lieben was at the counter ordering coffee, she removed her hands from the table and placed them on her lap so he wouldn't see them shaking. Adrenaline was coursing through her veins, making her tremble.

Lieben came over and took the seat opposite her. He smiled but it didn't reach his eyes. "Miss Lake, what a charming place you have chosen for our meeting."

Felicity shot him a smile that was every bit as fake as his own. "You said you had some information for Alec."

"Yes, I have some information for him," he said. "Also, I was hoping he might have some for me."

"Information for you?" Felicity asked.

Lieben took a sip of his coffee, nodded to himself in appreciation, and set the cup down gently on the table. "Yes, I was hoping for an exchange of information. When I tell him what I know about his father's disappearance, I was hoping he could enlighten me further."

"Alec doesn't know anything about his father's disappearance," Felicity said. "He can't help you with that."

"Perhaps he can once he knows what his father was working on just before he disappeared," Lieben said.

"What do you mean?" Felicity asked.

Lieben took another sip of coffee. "I've been investigating the disappearance of Thomas Harbinger and I've come to the conclusion that he was not kidnapped or taken against his will. He engineered his own disappearance."

"How can you possibly know that?" Felicity said.

"There were a number of people in Hyde Park that day," Lieben said. "Many of them were taking pictures and videos on their phones. Some inadvertently caught Thomas Harbinger's disappearance. "I have seen enough footage to convince me that Thomas cast some sort of spell that made him vanish from the park. He cast it himself. There was no one else around."

"And how do you think Alec can give you any more information on that?" Felicity asked. "Thomas may have disappeared on purpose but he hasn't visited Alec as far as I know."

Lieben nodded. "Perhaps he has not, but Alec may be able to throw some light on what Thomas was researching just before he disappeared and if that had anything to do with him going underground as you say."

"What do you mean? What was he researching?"

Lieben finished his coffee and said, "This was quite delicious. I most remember this place if I'm ever in Exeter again."

"Thomas's research?" Felicity prompted.

"Yes," Lieben said, "his research. It is most strange and it has is all baffled. Before he disappeared, Thomas was researching the death of his wife. That is strange is it not?"

"Perhaps," Felicity said. "But why do you think Alec could help you with that?"

"Alec was with his mother in the car, wasn't he? At the time of the accident I mean. Alec survived but his mother did not. He is the only witness of her death. Perhaps there is more surrounding that event than we know."

"I don't see how that could be," Felicity said. "And Alec was just a child at the time so I don't know how you think he can help you."

"He may remember more than he realizes," Lieben said. "After all, he has had problems with his memory before. The Paris incident for example."

"That's different," Felicity said. "His memories of Paris was stolen from him." She didn't mention that Alec now has those memories back; she wasn't sure how much Lieben knew about that.

"Yes, apparently they were," he said, "but the memories of his mother's death might simply be repressed in his mind. We have ways of helping him recover those memories."

Felicity had heard about their ways; Alec had told her that after Paris, he had been interrogated while being forced to wear a magical collar from the Spanish Inquisition that made him tell the truth. Was this what Lieben had in mind?

"I'm not sure why you think the circumstances surrounding Alec's mother's death are important now, after all this time," she said.

"Frankly, neither am I," he told her. "But the fact that Thomas Harbinger had a renewed interest in those events seems to indicate that they are important."

"Well, I can pass this information on to Alec," Felicity said, "but I'm not sure how much he'll be able to help you regarding the details of his mother's death. I was under the impression that the car crash was an accident."

"According to the Oregon police, it was," Lieben said, "but they were looking at the event from a mundane perspective. You and I both know that things are not always as they seem."

"So, do you have any of your own theories?" she asked.

He gave her an enigmatic smile. "Perhaps," was all he said.

"Well, I'll be sure to pass this on to Alec," Felicity said, giving her voice a touch of finality that she hoped would end this conversation.

She'd gotten the information she wanted out of Lieben, which wasn't much other than the fact that Thomas Harbinger had engineered his own disappearance. The fact that he'd been looking into his wife's death was interesting but Felicity couldn't see how it was relevant to anything.

"Thank you, Miss Lake, and be sure to tell Alec to contact me at his convenience. Also, I would like to be informed if Thomas tries to make contact with Alec, although I have a feeling I won't be, since Thomas seems determined to hide from the Society for some reason. And I'm sure Alec's loyalty to his father is stronger than his loyalty to the Society."

He pushed back his chair and stood. "I would ask you to inform me if Thomas makes contact, but I'm sure your loyalty to Alec is stronger than your loyalty to anyone."

Felicity didn't answer.

"Good day, Miss Lake," Lieben said before turning on his heels and leaving the coffee shop.

Felicity watched him through the window. A black Bentley pulled up to the curb and Lieben got in. The car pulled into the busy afternoon traffic and disappeared from view.

Felicity got up from the table and went to the bathroom at the back of the shop. When she got in there, she locked the door and rifled through her handbag until she found a waterproof eyeliner pencil. She lifted her sweater, exposing the skin of her stomach, and, using the pencil, drew a magical symbol of protection on herself. She might not have the tattoos that Alec sported, but this should keep her hidden from magical detection or scrying.

She still wasn't sure if she could trust Lieben or not but she'd decided she wasn't taking any chances.

CHAPTER 22

FOUR HOURS AFTER STEPPING THROUGH the portal in Blackthorn House, I was climbing out of a Ford Taurus that Leon had rented at Bangor International. The drive back to Dearmont had been quiet. I'd been mulling over how I was going to get my friends back from the clutches of the ancient vampires and I assumed Leon's thoughts ran along similar lines.

It was only ten-thirty when I got out of the Taurus in front of my house but I was beat. There was no point in going to see the Blackwell Sisters—who I believed could help us with our passport situation—until tomorrow so I looked in at Leon behind the wheel and said, "Meet me here at nine"

"Okay, see you soon," he said before pulling away from the curb.

I went inside and checked my phone. The damn thing wasn't working. It had acted strangely before after I'd been to Faerie but had eventually synced itself. Now, after a trip to the Shadow Land, it seemed to be broken.

I went upstairs, put the phone on the nightstand and connected the charger, and lay on the bed. I planned to wait for the phone to sort itself out and then I was going to leave a message for Mallory, telling her what I'd learned about Mister Scary. Then, I intended to call Felicity.

But as soon as my head hit the pillow, I fell asleep.

* * *

Leon arrived in his canary-yellow Porsche Cayman at nine and he looked better than I felt. Despite having spent fifteen minutes under a cold shower, I still felt groggy as I went outside. I was wearing shades because the day seemed too bright. I felt like I had a hangover and the color of the Porsche wasn't helping any.

"You ready to rock and roll?" he asked.

"No," I said, "but I don't have any choice. Leave your car here; we'll take the Land Rover."

He put his car into my driveway and I slid in behind the wheel of the Land Rover. As I drove toward town, Leon said, "Is your phone working? I think mine got fried by the Shadow Land."

"Mine isn't working either," I said. I'd tried it as soon as I'd woken up but, despite being charged up, it couldn't seem to find the network. I had it in my pocket anyway, just in case it decided to come alive again at some point. If not, I could use a payphone at the airport to call Mallory and Felicity.

"You said yesterday that the Blackwell Sisters can get our passports," Leon said. "How are they going to do that?"

"They can't get our passports but they can make us new ones," I said. "There's a magical technique where a piece of paper can be enchanted to look like anything you want. The Blackwell Sisters should be able to make us two enchanted passports that will get us to England."

"Okay, cool," he said.

By the time we pulled over outside Blackwell Books, I felt a little better. I climbed out and made my way into the bookshop.

At least the interior of the shop was gloomy. I removed my shades and hung them on my shirt pocket.

"Alec, how nice to see you." Victoria Blackwell appeared from behind a stack of books and came over to us. "And Leon too. To what do we owe the pleasure?" She was dressed in her usual attire, consisting of a long black lace dress that looked as if it was stylish maybe a hundred years ago.

"We need passports," I told her. "Or something that will look like passports, anyway."

She raised a quizzical eyebrow. "Oh? Are you going somewhere?"

"England," I said.

"Oh, how lovely. It can be a little cool at this time of year, so make sure you wrap up warm."

"We'll do that," I promised. "So can you make the passports?"

"Yes, yes, of course. Come with me." She led us to the back of the shop where she and her sister, Devon, had an office.

Devon was in the office, sitting at the desk in front of the computer. She looked up as we entered. "Alec! And Leon too. How nice of you to visit us!"

"Devon," I said, nodding. "It's nice to see you too."

"They want passports," Victoria told her sister.

"Passports? Are you going somewhere nice?"

"England," I said.

"For a vacation?"

"No, business."

"Well, it can be a little chilly there at this time of year, so make sure you—"

"Wrap up warm. Yes, we know. Don't worry about us."

"We can make the passports for you," Victoria said. "But are you sure that's how you want to travel? Flights can be so boring."

I frowned at her. "How else would we get there?"

She looked at Devon and an unspoken communication seemed to pass between them. Victoria looked back at me and said, "Where exactly are you going in England?"

"A place called Bodmin Moor in Cornwall."

Her face lit up. "Cornwall! Excellent! A place steeped in myth and legend. Yes, we can definitely help you get there."

Devon opened the desk drawer and took out an old leather-bound book. She began leafing through it and I could see hand-drawn maps on the pages. She stopped when she came to a page near the back of the book and traced her finger over the map until she found what she was looking for. She looked up at Victoria and said, "There's a stone circle in the area."

"We can transport you there," Victoria told me.

"You mean through some sort of portal?" I asked.

"Yes," Devon said, nodding enthusiastically. "It's something new we've been working on."

"Actually, it's something old. We discovered it in a spellbook," Victoria said. "We can transport you from here to any place where there's some sort of hallowed ground."

"Stone circles," Devon added. "Or old temples. And churches, of course."

I thought about that for a moment. I'd been through enough portals lately to last me a lifetime and I didn't have a burning desire to go through another. But it would be faster than catching a flight, and speed was of the essence. We had to get to that torc before Davos discovered its location.

"Okay," I said. "We need to get some stuff from the Land Rover first."

"Of course," Devon said excitedly. "We'll make preparations for the spell while you get your things."

I turned to leave the office, then stopped and turned back to face the witches. "You've done this before, right?"

"Don't you worry about that," Victoria said. "Now, go and get your luggage for the journey and meet us back here as soon as you can."

Leon and I went out to the Land Rover and I opened the back. After transferring my stuff from the trunk of Felicity's Mini a while ago and discovering that keeping my gear in a chaotic pile wasn't practical, I'd bought a large military duffel bag to hold the most important items. Inside, there were swords, daggers, faerie stones, crystal shards, a shotgun, bags of salt, wooden stakes, and a mallet. I heaved it out of the Land Rover and put it over my shoulder.

"This should be everything we need," I told him. "If we flew to England, I was going to get some supplies from the Society's headquarters but this way, we can use my stuff."

"Do you think this is safe?" Leon asked. "The witches sending us through a portal, I mean. The last time we went through a portal, the outcome wasn't so great."

"The sisters are a little eccentric," I told him, "but they know their stuff. We'll be fine." But even as I said it, I felt a twinge of reluctance. The witches did know their stuff, that was true, but I wasn't sure how many times they'd cast this portal spell before, if ever. Still, we had no quicker way of traveling to England and getting our hands on Gloria's torc.

The other thing that gave me pause was that the Blackwell Sisters hadn't demanded a payment for helping us. Usually, they made me to promise to return the favor but this time, they weren't concerned about payment for their services. That made me even more certain that Leon and I were being used as lab rats for the transportation spell.

We went back into the bookshop and made our way between the bookshelves to the office. The Blackwell sisters weren't there.

"This way," Devon called to us from deeper within the shop. We followed her through a door marked PRIVATE and along a short corridor to a small room where a magical circle had been painted on the floor in red paint. The circle was ringed by burning white candles that provided the only light in the room.

An altar sat at one end of the room, covered with a black cloth that had a white pentagram embroidered on it. On the altar sat a small cauldron that didn't have a heat source beneath it but was giving off a thick, pungent smoke that smelled of marigolds and hawthorn berries.

Victoria was standing in front of the altar, consulting a spell book.

Leon and I walked into the circle and I dropped the duffel bag at our feet.

"Got everything you need?" Victoria asked, looking up from the book.

"Yeah," I said.

"Not quite everything," Devon said, smiling. "I'll be back in a moment." She left the room.

"How do we get back here when we're ready to come home?" I asked Victoria.

"Just give us a call," she said. "You have our number. As long as you're standing on hallowed ground somewhere—anywhere in the world—we can bring you back here."

Devon came back into the room, carrying two oversized dark blue knitted sweaters. "You might need these," she said. "Here, take them."

Leon and I took the sweaters. They were large enough that we could both have worn the same one and still have room to spare.

"We knitted them ourselves," Devon said proudly.

"Great, thanks," I said, dropping mine onto the duffel bag. Leon did the same and the bag disappeared beneath a sea of dark blue wool.

"Ready to go?" Victoria asked.

We nodded.

"Whatever happens, don't leave the circle until the spell is done. Hopefully, by then, you'll be standing on Bodmin Moor."

"Hopefully?" I said.

213

She grinned. "I told you not to worry, Alec. You look worried."

"I'm fine," I said. "Let's just get on with it."

Devon went behind the altar and picked up a silver bowl that contained leaves and herbs, as well as two small daggers. She came into the circle and handed Leon and me a dagger each. She held the bowl in both hands, out toward us, and said, "You both need to put a drop of blood in here."

I nicked my finger and squeezed a drop of blood onto the herbs. Leon did the same with his dagger. Devon took the bowl and daggers back to the altar and began reciting words in a language I was unfamiliar with. Victoria was also speaking in what sounded like a second unknown language.

I felt my hair stand on end as the energy within the circle began to increase. It felt like it was swirling around us, creating a vortex. The sisters chanted faster, the words of the two different languages seeming to deflect off one another and echo around the room.

Devon tipped the contents of the silver bowl into the cauldron on the altar. The smoke turned bright red for a second and then it was gone.

The entire room was gone.

Leon and I stood outside in the center of a circle of standing stones. By the appearance of the cloudy sky, I guessed it was early evening, maybe an hour or so before nightfall. The landscape around us was flat and green, dotted here and there with stands of trees and low hills, with a village in the distance. The air was cold.

"Wow, they did it," Leon said.

I nodded. "Yeah, they did. And they were right about the weather." I took one of the knitted sweaters off the duffel bag and put it on. It drowned me and I had to roll up the sleeves just to see my hands but at least it was warm.

Leon put on his sweater and, because he was smaller-framed than me, had to roll up the bottom of it because it reached past his knees. "Who did they knit these for? Giants?"

My phone buzzed in my pocket, surprising me. The trip through the portal must have shocked it back into life. I answered it.

The voice on the other end was Victoria Blackwell's. "Are you there? Did it work?"

"Yeah, we're here," I said. "The spell worked. I guess that's why you're calling, to make sure we weren't blown into a thousand pieces or something."

"Excellent!" she said. "Devon, it worked!" In the background, I heard Devon whoop with joy. Then Victoria said, "You call us the moment you're ready to return and we'll bring you back here immediately. Isn't our spell wonderful?"

"Well, we're still alive, so there's that, I guess. I'll call you later. Bye." I ended the call then looked at my phone. I had texts from Felicity asking where I was and a number of voicemail messages that I assumed were also from her. I called her.

When she answered, her voice held a mixture of worry and relief. "Alec! I've been so worried. Where are you? Are you all right?"

"I'm fine. Leon is with me but the others have been captured by the Midnight Cabal."

"Oh my God! Are you going to rescue them?"

"We're working on it. We're trying to find the torc that gives Gloria her power. Listen, can you get a car and meet us here? We 're in the middle of nowhere right now."

There was a slight pause and then Felicity said, "Of course. I'll get the first flight I can—"

"No, you don't have to do that. We're in England."

"What? How? No, never mind, you can tell me later. I can pick you up, I've got my dad's Volvo. Where exactly are you?"

"We're standing in the center of a stone circle on Bodmin Moor."

There was another pause. "All right. Do you know which stone circle? There are more than one there."

I looked at Leon, who was playing with his phone. "Is your GPS working?"

"Way ahead of you," he said. "This stone circle is called The Hurlers and that village over there is called Minions."

"We'll be at a village called Minions," I told Felicity.

"All right. It should take me about an hour to get there."

"I'll see you later," I said.

She ended the call.

Leon said, "There a few bodies of water around here but how are we supposed to know which one is the right one?"

"Good question. Gloria had said she gave the torc to her sister in the Middle Ages. Maybe the lake isn't even here anymore. We'll ask at the village." I swung the duffel bag over my shoulder. The contents clanked together, then settled as I walked out of the stone circle and across the moor.

"You ever been to England before?" I asked Leon as we walked toward the distant huddle of buildings.

"A couple of times but I've only been to London. It was nothing like this. This landscape is pretty bleak."

As we got closer to the village, I spotted a place that would be the perfect for questioning the locals. I pointed it out to Leon, a large stone building with wooden picnic tables set out in front of it. A sign over the door displayed a painting of the stone circle with the words The Hurler's Arms.

"A pub," Leon said, grinning. "I like your thinking."

Five minutes later, we entered The Hurler's Arms. The place looked old, with exposed wooden beams in the low ceiling and a huge stone fireplace dominating one wall. A small fire burned quietly, lending an aroma of wood-smoke to the smell of hops that filled the room.

The windows were small, admitting only the barest amount of light from the outside, so the room was lit by lamps set in the walls. Paintings of the wild moor hung over the fireplace.

I assumed the pub would get busy later but right now, the only patrons were a couple of old men in dark trousers, boots, and gray knitted sweaters sitting at a table near the fire with pints of dark beer.

The barman was in his fifties with gray hair and a neatly-cropped beard. He looked over at us as we entered. "What can I get you, gentlemen?"

I looked at the names of the beers on the taps. "Two pints of Doom Bar, please. Do you take plastic?" We didn't have any British money on us, a drawback to traveling via Blackwell Airlines.

"Of course, mate." He grabbed a portable card machine and put it on the bar in front of me while he poured the beers.

When we had our drinks and I'd paid for them, Leon and I took them over to a table by the fireplace, next to the two men who looked like locals.

"Afternoon," I said as we passed them.

They looked up from their pints but didn't say anything.

"Looks like a tough crowd," Leon whispered as we took our seats.

But one of the men looked over and said, "We don't get many of your type in here."

218

I raised an eyebrow at him. "Our type?"

"Americans."

"We're here to see the lake," I said.

"What lake might that be?" the other man asked.

"There's only one lake around here surrounded by legend, isn't there?" I asked. If the lake Gloria had mentioned did exist, and if it was inhabited by a faerie, there was sure to be a legend surrounding the place.

The first man grinned. "Hear that, Bernie? They've come all the way from the States to see Dozmary Pool."

The man named Bernie nodded, his rheumy eyes traveling from Leon to me and back to Leon again. "I heard what he said, George. Maybe they're treasure hunters, come here looking for Excalibur."

"Excalibur?" Leon asked. "*The* Excalibur?"

George nodded. "Dozmary Pool is where the Lady of the Lake gave Excalibur to King Arthur. It's also where Sir Bedivere threw the sword after Arthur's death."

"But just as the blade was about to hit the water," Bernie said, "the Lady of the Lake's hand came up out of the pool and caught it before sinking back down into the depths, sword and all. You're not here looking for treasure, are you?"

"No," I said. "But that's the lake we want to take a look at. It's somewhere near here, isn't it?"

"It's around these parts," Bernie said, "but you don't want to be going there, especially not this late in the day, in case you get lost on the moor at night."

"Because then, Tregeagle will come for you," George added.

"Tregeagle?" I asked. I knew these men were telling us the local legends but I also knew that if there was a legend of something out on the moor that came for people in the night, it was probably based on fact.

"Tregeagle the giant," Bernie said. "The guardian of the pool. On a cold winter's night, when you can hear the wind howling over the moor, you can sometimes hear something else as well, something howling that isn't the wind. That's Tregeagle, roaming Bodmin Moor, tortured by the demons that haunt him."

"But I don't expect you yanks to believe any of that," George said. "You probably think it's just superstitious nonsense told by old men who have nothing better to do than tell tall tales."

"You'd be surprised," I said.

There was a pause while we all took a sip of our beer, then Bernie said, "Did you really come here to see Dozmary Pool?"

"Yes, we did," Leon said. "Can you tell us where it is?"

"Ten miles or so that way," George said, pointing out of the window at Bodmin Moor. "You can drive almost all the way up to it if your car can handle a few bumps and potholes."

"Just make sure you don't drive into the pool itself," Bernie said, chuckling.

"Thanks," I said, raising my beer to them. They went back to their own conversation and I said to Leon, "That must be the place we're looking for."

He'd been typing on his phone. Now, he showed me a map on the screen. "They're right, Dozmary Pool is eleven miles east of here."

"As soon as Felicity arrives, we'll drive over there," I said.

"Do you think the Lady of the Lake will just give us the torc?"

I shrugged. "Maybe, if I can convince her we need it to save her sister. I just hope this isn't going to involve making a bargain with another faerie." I took a big sip of my beer.

"Hey, maybe she'll just give it to you," Leon said. "She gave Excalibur to King Arthur and didn't get anything in return. Maybe she'll know what you need the torc for and hand it over."

"Yeah, somehow I don't think it's going to be that simple. And then there's the guardian of the pool."

"You think he's real?"

I put my half-drained glass onto the table. "The legend came from somewhere. Bernie and George probably like scaring tourists with the tale of Tregeagle and probably don't believe it themselves but you and I know that the idea of a giant living somewhere on that moor isn't so far-fetched."

"Yeah, you got that right."

We drank in silence for a while and I pulled up some websites on Dozmary Pool. Outside, a light rain began to fall and Bodmin Moor became shrouded in mist and darkness.

I wondered if Gloria had revealed the location of the torc to the vampires yet. Would we get to the lake only to find that the vamps had already been there and taken the torc, giving the Midnight Cabal enough power to take over the parts of Faerie they needed to launch their attack on the Society?

A thought struck me. "They must be in this realm."

Leon, who had been looking out of the window at the rain, turned to me. "What's that?"

"The vamps. They must have brought Gloria to this realm for questioning. The time dilation that occurs between here and the faerie realm means that even if they got the information out of her in a day in Faerie, weeks might have passed here. They probably suspect we know the location of the torc and wouldn't allow us that much time to go ahead and find it. So they must have Gloria here somewhere. That's the only way they can ensure that if a day passes for them, it's only a day for us too."

Leon shrugged. "Okay, but where? They could be anywhere in the world."

"True, but if they're in this realm, at least they'll be easier to find than if they were still in Faerie."

"Yeah, I guess." He pointed out of the window. "Felicity's here."

A silver Volvo SUV pulled up into the parking lot, Felicity behind the wheel. I grabbed the duffel bag and we left the pub, nodding a farewell to Bernie and George who were still nursing their pints by the fireplace.

Outside, the night had turned even cooler. The rain fell in an insidious drizzle and the mist-shrouded moor looked forbidding. It was easy to see how legends of giants and faerie-inhabited lakes had become associated with this place.

I opened the trunk of the Volvo and threw the duffel bag in before going around to the passenger side and getting in quickly before the rain seeped through the knitted sweater. Leon climbed into the back.

"How did you know we'd be at the pub?" I asked Felicity as I closed my door.

"There aren't many other places you could be," she said.

"We need to go to a lake called Dozmary Pool," I told her. "It's near here." I read the postcode off my phone and Felicity typed it into the Volvo's GPS.

As she backed away from the pub, she asked, "How long have you been in England?"

"A little over an hour."

When she looked at me with a confused look in her dark eyes, I said, "I'll explain on the way."

CHAPTER 23

By the time we got to Dozmary Pool, Leon and I had filled Felicity in on the events that had occurred since the demons had attacked us in Canada. She'd listened intently, driving us along a narrow road that ran through Bodmin Moor and then a rough track that led to the lake. When the track ended fifty yards from the water's edge, Felicity hit the brakes and killed the engine.

Dozmary Pool was a roughly-circular body of water that, according to the websites, was a mile in circumference but the mist that hung over the water and the moor obscured the opposite bank so as I looked at the lake through the Volvo's windshield, it looked like it could stretch into the mysterious distance forever. There was a small rowboat on the bank that had once been painted bright blue but now the paint had mostly flaked away.

I got out of the car, my boots sinking slightly into the wet ground, and went to the back to get the weapons. The guardian of the pool might be no more than an old legend but I wasn't taking any chances.

Leon and Felicity joined me at the rear of the vehicle as I opened up the bag and took out three swords in leather scabbards. I gave one each to Leon and Felicity and took the third for myself, attaching it to my belt. I also handed out faerie stones in case there was some sort of veiling spell over the pool. Then, I closed the trunk and walked across the sodden ground to the water's edge.

None of us had spoken since arriving here. An aura of solemnity seemed to surround the place and I felt that if I spoke, my voice would sound too loud, shattering the solemn silence and warning something of our presence here. The only sound was the gentle hiss of rain falling into the lake.

I was drenched after only a couple of minutes, the oversized sweater clinging to me like a cold, wet blanket, the rain water soaking through to my shirt and my skin beneath that.

Leon and Felicity were in the same state. The three of us must have looked like drowned rats as we trudged through the mud to the edge of the lake.

I raised my faerie stone to my eyes and looked out across the water. There was definitely magic in this place; through the hole in the stone, the mist looked as if it were shot through with bright blue veins of pulsing energy. But

225

apart from that, I couldn't see anything else. If Gloria's sister was here, she was probably hidden beneath the water.

I felt suddenly foolish. Had I thought that Vivian, the Lady of the Lake, would reveal herself and give the torc to me just because I was trying to help her sister? She didn't know why I was here or what my motives were.

Despite my reticence to make a sound, I was about to call out across the water and tell the faerie why I was here, when something caught my attention. A low groan came drifting to my ears from somewhere on the hidden moor.

Leon and Felicity heard it too and we turned to face the direction the sound had come from. Another groan sounded, this one closer. It sounded like a man in agony.

Then I saw a hulking shape in the mist, at least twenty feet tall. It was a red-haired giant wielding a huge club. He had a long red beard that reached down over the front of his studded leather tunic. He looked down on us and groaned again, as if it was the only sound he could make.

I drew my sword, the blade igniting blue as soon as it left the scabbard. Leon and Felicity drew their weapons too and we stood facing the giant.

"Tregeagle," I said, "we aren't here to hurt you. We're trying to help the Lady of the Lake's sister, the Lady of the Forest. She's in danger and we need her torc to give her back her power so she can reclaim her home."

He stepped forward, lifting the club above his head, a look of anger in his eyes.

We scattered as the blow came down, the heavy club burying itself in the mud where we'd been standing. Tregeagle roared in frustration when he saw we'd avoided his attack.

I leaped forward and sliced the blade of my sword across his thigh, drawing blood. The giant released his grip on the club and swung a huge hand at me, trying to swat me away. The edge of his hand caught me and the wind was knocked out of me as I was thrown through the air. I landed in the lake, splashing into the cold water and getting a mouthful of it before scrambling back to my feet.

The giant's attention had turned to Leon and as he stepped forward, he pulled the club out of the mud and readied himself for another attack.

Felicity darted behind the giant and swung her sword at the back of his legs. The enchanted blade bit into the giant's thigh. Tregeagle howled in pain, his attack on Leon forgotten, and twisted around to face Felicity. She stepped back, her glowing sword held aloft in a defensive position.

There was no way her blade was going to protect her from the weight of the giant's club. Tregeagle swung the club over his head and down toward Felicity. She threw herself to one side, avoiding the blow and rolling to safety.

I ran out of the lake and toward the giant but stopped when more shapes appeared in the mist. The newcomers were human-sized and, as they stepped into view, I realized they were demons. There were a dozen of them and they were trailing behind Davos.

When he saw me, the vampire grinned wickedly. "Alec, you're here. I must admit to being slightly disappointed that you beat us here but we had to wait until sundown. After the faerie queen told us where the torc was hidden, I'd hoped we'd get it and be long gone by the time you arrived."

"What have you done with the Lady of the Forest?" I demanded.

"She's alive. For now, at least. I had to keep her alive in case this lake she told us about wasn't the actual location of the torc. But the fact that you're here tells me she wasn't lying. So she can be destroyed later. Her usefulness to me has ended."

"And what about my friends?"

His grin widened. "They mean nothing to me, Alec. They're alive at the moment but they won't be for long. Maybe you'd like to watch them die, along with the faerie?"

"I'd rather watch you die," I said, summoning a magical bolt into my hand. The energy crackled around my fingers.

Davos sighed as if bored. "Very well." He looked at his demon minions and indicated us with a flick of his fingers. "Kill them."

The demons rushed forward, past their vampire master. Felicity and Leon readied themselves and Tregeagle seemed to have decided that the demons were a more urgent threat than us three. He roared and waded into the red-skinned bodies, swinging his club.

I threw my arm forward and released the magical bolt at Davos. The energy arced through the air and exploded when it hit the vampire's body. He staggered backward but managed to stay on his feet. Before he had a chance to recover, I ran at him with my sword held steady before me, ready to run him through with it.

He waited until I was almost upon him and moved out of the way with blinding speed. One moment he was in front of my blade, the next, he was behind me, grabbing my throat with hands as cold as the grave.

"I should have choked the life out of you last time," he said calmly, "but I decided instead to respect the wishes of the Cabal. I won't make the same mistake twice."

I had no idea who in the Cabal wanted me spared and it looked like I'd never know as Davos's grip around my throat tightened. I looked over at Leon and Felicity, fighting the demons alongside Tregeagle, and wanted to tell them to get away from here.

But not only was Davos squeezing the life out of me, the weakness that came as a side effect of using my magic was flooding my limbs, making it feel as if all my strength was ebbing away into the mud beneath my feet.

Davos must have detected my sudden weakness because he loosened his grip slightly. "Don't die on me too soon, Alec. Surely you want to see your friends defeated by my demons before you leave this mortal coil."

I didn't even have the strength to struggle as he turned my face toward the fray at the edge of the pool. The defeat he was looking for didn't seem to be happening, though; Leon, Felicity, and the giant were holding their own against the demons. In fact, they were winning. Six demons lay dead at the water's edge and the remaining six didn't look as if they posed any threat. They fought sloppily and were being cut down by swords and crushed by the giant's club.

Davos sighed. "No matter. I'll kill your friends myself. But first I'll deal with you." He tightened his grip again.

The red unicursal hexagram appeared in my mind's eye. I concentrated on it as intently as I could. Davos didn't technically have a life force so I had no idea how the magic would affect him, if at all, but I had to try. At least I might get enough strength back to struggle from his grasp.

The lack of oxygen was making me lightheaded but I fixed my attention on the magical symbol as strongly as I could.

I heard Davos say, "What's happening?" He sounded confused, maybe even scared.

His grip around my throat loosened slightly and something else happened that surprised me; his hands grew warm as if blood was being pumped through his veins.

"No," he said, releasing me and stepping back. "What are you doing?"

I turned to face him. He was looking down at his own body as if it were alien to him. His skin, normally as white as alabaster, had become like a living person's. He looked up at me with fear in his eyes and I understood what had happened. The magic had drawn the life force from around me and, somehow, because he was a vampire with no life force of his own, Davos had absorbed some of it. He'd become partly human again.

Hopefully, human enough to kill.

I picked up my sword and swung it at him. He tried to dodge out of the way but his speed had deserted him. The enchanted blade bit into his shoulder and carried on into his chest. Davos screamed. I pulled the sword from his flesh and swung it again, this time taking off his head.

The body collapsed to the ground next to the severed head and then the stolen life force seemed to drain from them both and they returned to the pale white of the vampire. Then they crumbled into dust before my eyes, leaving behind only Davos's suit in the mud.

"What the hell happened?" Leon said from behind me.

I turned to see him and Felicity standing there with demon blood on their swords. A dozen scarlet-skinned bodies lay by the lake.

"My magic made him temporarily human," I said. "Some of the life force that was supposed to aid my recovery went into him."

"Wow," Leon said.

"Where's Tregeagle?" I asked, looking for the giant.

"He left after we killed the demons," Felicity said. "He just vanished into the mist."

I walked over to the water's edge and looked across the misty surface. "Vivian, Lady of the Lake," I called, "if you're there, you must know from what happened here that we're trying to help your sister. She needs the torc she gave to you for safekeeping. There are other vampires and demons that mean to do your sister harm. Help us to help her by giving us the torc."

The mist swallowed my words. I stood looking out over the water for a couple of minutes longer but nothing happened.

"Perhaps this is the wrong lake after all," Felicity said, coming up beside me.

"Or maybe the Lady of the Lake has moved somewhere else," Leon suggested.

"No," I said, "she has to be here. The guardian was here so she should be too."

"Perhaps not all legends are true," Felicity said.

"This one is. I know it. This pool has been associated with the Lady of the Lake for centuries. She has to be here."

There was a sudden splash on the lake. I looked out to see a woman's hand thrust up from beneath the water. In the hand was a bright golden torc, its open end pointing toward the sky. Rivulets of water ran down over the torc and over the chainmail-clad forearm and hand that held it.

The arm didn't move, simply remained where it was out on the lake, offering the torc.

I ran over to the old rowboat and pushed it out onto the water, jumping in and rowing out to where the Lady of the Lake waited. When I reached the outstretched arm, I peered below the water. It was murky down there but I saw blond hair, silver chain mail and the form of a woman.

I reached out for the torc and, as I grasped it, the Lady of the Lake's hand slipped beneath the surface of the water again.

I sat back in the boat and examined the torc. It was finely-crafted, made to look like three intertwining golden braids. The braids curved in a U-shape and terminated in two small golden discs set with emeralds.

I rowed back to shore and showed it to Felicity and Leon.

"It's beautiful," Felicity said, holding the torc on the palm of her hand and looking at it with wide eyes .

I nodded. "Now, we just need to find out where they're holding Gloria and the others. Davos said they weren't too far from here."

Felicity said, "Alec, look." She nodded to the torc on her palm.

"What?" I asked.

"It just moved."

"Are you sure?"

"Yes, it moved on my hand." She moved her hand to the left. The torc moved slightly so that its open end was pointing in the same direction it had been before Felicity had moved.

"It's like a divining rod," Felicity said.

"Yeah, and I bet I know what it's pointing at. It's obviously connected to Gloria. Let's put it on the dash in the Volvo and see where it takes us. We'll find Gloria and the others by faerie GPS."

CHAPTER 24

I PUT THE SWORDS IN the trunk while Felicity got into the Volvo and placed the torc on the dash. A silvery quality to the night air told me the moon was out even though I couldn't see it through the mist. When I got into the Volvo, the torc was pointing west across Bodmin Moor, toward the coast.

"I can't just drive over the moor," Felicity said. "I'll have to find the proper roads to get us where we want to go." She turned the Volvo around and drove back along the track toward the road. The torc revolved on the dash, pointing behind us until Felicity got onto the road and did a U-turn to point us in the right direction.

As we headed west, the torc didn't move. I put the heating on full blast; maybe we'd manage to dry off before we had to go out into the rain again.

"This must be the right direction," Felicity said. "Since the torc seems to be pointing directly at Gloria as the crow flies, what's dead ahead of us?" She pointed at the glove compartment. "My dad keeps a road map in there."

I opened the glove compartment and got the map book out, turning on the overhead light and leafing through the book until I found Bodmin Moor. I found the road we were on and traced my finger across the page in a westerly direction. "There's nothing but fields, then cliffs and a beach."

"Maybe there's a cave in the cliffs," Leon suggested. "The vamps would have had to stay out of the sun while they waited for it to set. A cave would be ideal."

"Yeah, it would," I agreed.

Felicity nodded. "I'll head for the cliffs unless the torc suddenly changes direction."

I turned off the overhead light but kept the map book on my lap in case it was needed again. Half an hour later, we reached a coastal road that ran north to south. On the other side of the road, the tops of the cliffs were visible in the headlights and, beyond that, the lights of boats twinkling over the dark sea.

The torc pointed directly out at them.

"Maybe they're not on the beach," I said. "Maybe they're on a boat."

Felicity drove across the coastal road and parked the Volvo on the cliff top. "We'll need to find a way down there whether they're on the beach or a boat."

We got out of the car and got the swords out of the back. Leaving them in their scabbards so their enchanted glow didn't give us away, we walked along the rain-swept cliffs, looking for a way down to the beach. There was no mist here and the sky was starlit, with a half-moon shining down on us.

When we found a steep, rock-strewn path that cut through the cliff and descended to the beach below, we took it, and ten minutes later we were standing on a wide stretch of sand. The sea crashed onto the beach with the rhythm of a heartbeat. The air tasted salty.

I looked out to sea, then at the torc resting on Felicity's open palm. It pointed southeast.

"Looks like they *are* on a boat after all," Leon said.

I thought about it and then shook my head. "No, I don't think so. The torc points in Gloria's direction but it doesn't give any indication of how far away she is. Think about where we are on a map of the world. This is the southeast coast of England. If you traveled that way," I pointed out to sea in a south-easterly direction, "where would you end up?"

"France, if you went far enough," Felicity said.

"And beyond that?" I asked.

"Italy."

"A little farther," I said.

She though for a moment then said, "Greece."

I nodded. "Most vamps have a nostalgic connection to the place they called home before they were turned, the place they lived their life. It would make sense for ancient Greek vampires to have a lair somewhere in Greece, probably on Crete or one of the islands surrounding it."

"So you think that's where they're holding Jim and the others," Leon said. He nodded. "Yeah, that makes sense."

"I can do some research," Felicity said. "See if there are any islands with old dwellings on them that might serve as a vampire lair. But even if we find out exactly where they are, how are we going to get there?"

"The same way Leon and I got here," I said.

CHAPTER 25

FELICITY DROVE US BACK INLAND and found a place to park the Volvo near the stone circle. We all got out and I slung the duffel bag over my shoulder. The Hurlers Stone Circle was an eerie place at night, surrounded by mist. As we walked among the stones, I got out my phone and called Victoria Blackwell.

She answered immediately. "Alec," she said gleefully. "How nice to hear from you so soon."

"We need an exit," I said, quoting The Matrix.

"Of course," she said. "Are you in the same stone circle?"

"Yes," I said. "There are three of us now."

"That's not a problem," she said. "Devon and I will begin the spell immediately."

We waited. After a couple of minutes, the air within the stone circle seemed to become electric. I felt the hairs on my arms bristle. There seemed to be a humming coming from the stones themselves, and the faint blue light whirling around us like a tornado. The light became more vivid and bright until it filled my vision and I could see nothing else. Then, it faded just as quickly as it had grown in intensity and we were standing in the back room of Blackwell books again. There was a strong smell of incense in the air. Victoria and Devon was standing by the altar, beaming at us.

"We're so glad you're back safely," Victoria said, "and you brought Felicity too. How nice."

"Yeah, your spell works like a charm," I said.

Victoria looked at me with confusion in her eyes. "It isn't a charm, Alec, it's a translocation spell that is hundreds of years old."

"Figure of speech," I said. Then I thought better of trying to explain it to her and added, "Never mind. We may need you to send us somewhere else soon. Will you be able to do that?"

"Of course," Victoria said, "just let us know when you're ready to travel again."

"I will," I told her. "Thanks for your help."

We left the back room and went through the shop to the street where the Land Rover was parked. When we got in and I started the engine, I looked over at Blackwell Books and saw the sisters standing in the window waving at us. Felicity waved back and as she did so, she asked me, "What did you have to promise them this time?"

"Nothing," I said, "because this time we were helping them by being their lab rats."

Her dark eyes widened with surprise. "You mean they haven't cast that spell before?"

"That's right," I told her. "We're the first people to travel that way in a long time and I don't think the sisters were sure it was going to work." I pulled away from the curb and headed for home.

CHAPTER 26

WHEN WE GOT BACK TO my house, I went into the kitchen to grab three beers from the fridge and order a pizza. Felicity took a seat on the sofa in the living room with my laptop on the coffee table in front of her, her fingers flying over the keyboard. The torc sat on the table near the computer, resolutely pointing east.

Leon was on his cellphone trying to get Michael to postpone the rest of his vacation and come help us on the rescue mission. From the snatches of conversation I caught, it sounded like Leon was promising to make up the vacation time to Michael by letting him take it at a later date. I didn't think he was going to have a problem convincing his butler to join us because Michael seemed like the type of guy who thrived on action, much like Leon himself.

When I'd ordered the pizza and opened the beers, I went into the living room and sat down next to Felicity "How's it going?" I asked.

"It may take some time to sort through all the documents relating to the properties on the Greek islands around Crete," she said "but I'm sure I'll find something leads us to the vampires."

"I know you will," I said. "I have every faith in you."

She smiled at me but I detected coldness in it. No, not coldness but an emotional distance, as if she were putting up an unseen barrier between us.

I guessed that was totally understandable; her father had recently had a heart attack and was still recovering. Felicity probably thought that she should be still in England caring for him and not stuck on my living room sofa researching vampires, a job that she could have done just as easily from her parents' house.

"Listen," I said. "When we came back through the portal, I just assumed you'd want to come with us. I didn't think that you might want to go back to Sussex. I'm sorry."

She looked surprised for a moment. "What? No, I wanted to come. I want to be part of this." She pushed her glasses up the bridge of her nose. "Anyway, I'm assuming the witches will be able to send me back afterward."

"Of course they will," I said, feeling relieved that I hadn't forced her here against her will but still confused by the distance I felt between us.

"Alec, there's something I need to tell you," she said. "The reason I was in Exeter was because I went there to meet a man named Hans Lieben from the society." "

"Lieben," I said. "I've been trying to contact him. Some of the messages on my phone are probably from him but I haven't had a chance to check them yet."

"He has some information for you," Felicity said. "He told me that your father disappeared on purpose and that the last thing he was investigating before his disappearance was your mother's death. Don't you find that strange?"

"Not really. I was asking him about the car accident recently. I wanted to know if he genuinely thought my mother's death was accidental and not a murder, which my recent memories seem to suggest. As far as I could tell, he believed the accident story. Maybe my questions prompted him to look into is a little deeper."

"But then why did he disappear?" she asked.

I shrugged. "I don't know. That's something I'll have to ask him when he contacts me."

"Do you think he will? Contact you, I mean."

"If he uncovers some new information about my mother's death, I'm sure he will. At least, I hope so."

Felicity nodded and pointed at the laptop. "I should get back to this."

"Yeah," I said, putting a beer on the table in front of her and getting up. "I'll see if Leon has convinced Michael to help us."

I found Leon on the kitchen, putting his phone in his pocket.

"Any luck?" I asked, handing him a beer.

He nodded. "Yeah, Michael is glad to help. He should be here soon."

"Great. We're going to need all the help we can get if we're going to storm the vampires' lair."

Leon took a swig of beer. "That's assuming Felicity can find it. Those guys have had hundreds of years experience of covering their tracks."

"She'll find it," I said.

As if on cue, Felicity called from the living room, "I think I've found it."

We went over to the sofa to see what she'd discovered.

"There's an island called Dia," she said. "It's close to Santorini, which is where a volcano erupted three and a half thousand years ago and caused the catastrophe that some scholars think wiped out the Minoans. There's a ruined village on the island of Dia and also," she turned the laptop so Leon and I could see the screen, "this mansion."

The mansion was built on the cliffs, overlooking the sea and other islands in the distance. Built of stone with huge windows to capture the views, it didn't look like the kind of place vampires would choose to live.

"Those windows are very big," I said. "Not exactly the preferred architectural style for vampires who go crispy in the sunlight."

"There are legend surrounding this island," Felicity said. "The local sailors won't go near it. They say the residents only come out at night. The village on the island has been in ruins since it was apparently destroyed by monsters that decimated the residents during the course of a single night three hundred years ago. As for the windows on the mansion, look a bit closer at the picture."

I leaned in and nodded. "This is definitely the place." The windows were fitted with steel shutters on the inside and all those shutters were closed, blocking out every last ray of sunshine. "Felicity, can you check if there was a church in that village? If so, the Blackwell sisters can get us there."

She nodded and turned the laptop back around so she could see the screen. Her fingers flew over the keyboard again.

The pizza arrived and I went to the door to pay the delivery guy. As he was leaving, a blue Ford Bronco pulled up outside the house and Michael got out. "Good afternoon, sir," he said when he saw me.

"Hi, Michael. Thanks for cutting your vacation short."

"Not a problem, sir. I'm always willing to help however I can." He followed me into the house and said hello to Leon and Felicity.

"Did you bring the shotguns?" Leon asked him.

"Of course, sir."

I put the pizzas on the coffee table and opened the boxes. The house suddenly smelled of melted cheese and pepperoni. I got Michael a beer from the fridge and the four of us sat around the coffee table eating and drinking.

"I've found a church on the island," Felicity said. She was eating but put up a hand to cover her mouth while she spoke. "There's nothing left of it except for a couple of walls, though."

"That's fine," I said. "As long as it's hallowed ground, the transportation spell should work."

I called Victoria Blackwell. "Hey," I said when she answered. "We need to get to a Greek island called Dia. There's an old, ruined church there." I heard her relate the information to Devon.

"We're just looking it up now, Alec," she said. "How is everything else? All right? How were the sweaters?"

"Great. They kept us very warm."

"Well, that is good. You and Leon can keep them, you know. Consider them a gift from us."

"Thanks," I said.

Devon said something in the background and then Victoria said, "Yes, we can get you to that island. Isn't our spell wonderful?"

"It is," I said. "You'll be helping a lot of people. Some of our friends are being held in a vampire lair on that island."

"Oh? Anyone we know? It's not your friend Mallory is it? Or that lovely deputy, Amy Cantrell?"

"No, it isn't them. One of my old colleagues, a couple of Canadian cops, and a faerie queen."

She gasped. "A faerie queen? Which one?"

"I don't know. She goes by the title Lady of the Forest. At the moment, she's calling herself Gloria, but I know that isn't her real name."

"The Lady of the Forest!" Victoria said excitedly. In the background, I heard Devon give a whoop of excitement.

"You know her?" I asked.

"No, not personally, but we invoke her name sometimes when we do faerie magic. You say she's in danger?"

"That's right. We're going to go rescue her from some vampires and demons."

"Well, come over right away. Whenever you're ready."

"Thanks. I was thinking we'd wait until midnight. That way, because of the time difference between here and Crete, we'd arrive at sunrise."

"Ah, yes, of course," she said. "Hit the vampires during daylight. Well, we'll be here at midnight, ready to send you on your way."

"Thanks." I ended the call and turned to the others. "It seems the Blackwell sisters are a little star struck where Gloria is concerned. Anyway, they can get us onto the island."

"Do we have a plan after that, sir?" Michael asked.

I shrugged. "Not really. We need to get into that house and find Gloria and the others. I'd planned to take the torc to her and give it to her there so she could help us blast our way out of there but I think that's too risky. No need to take the torc right to our enemy's door. We'll leave it in the Land Rover and give it to Gloria when we get back to the bookshop."

"So we're going to hit them head-on?" Leon asked.

"I don't really see that we have much of a choice. We can try to get in using stealth, sure, but once we're discovered, it's going to turn real nasty real quick. We don't know how many demons are in there. Not to mention the two ancient vampires; Korax and Damalis. We're going to have a battle on our hands."

"You can take out the vamps the same way you took out Davos," Leon suggested.

"Maybe," I said, "but it's risky. I have to expend nearly all of my energy to do it and I can't predict how long it will take before the life-force regeneration thing happens. And what if one of you guys is too close at the time? We can't rely on my magic as a viable strategy. We're going to have to go old school and that means wooden stakes and decapitation."

Turning to Leon and Michael, I said, "I've got some shotgun cartridges that have wood mixed in with the metal shot. We can load the shotguns with those."

"And swords," Felicity said. "We need to take swords. Cutting off a vampire's head is a tried and true method of destroying it."

"We'll take swords," I said. "Let's finish the pizza and get the weapons ready. We've got a date with two ancient creatures that aren't going to die easily."

CHAPTER 27

WE ARRIVED AT BLACKWELL BOOKS at midnight. The sisters were waiting for us inside the door and when they saw us, they both smiled widely.

"There are four of us this time," I explained to the witches as Felicity, Leon, Michael, and I piled through the door with our weapons. "That won't be a problem will it?"

"Of course not," Victoria said. "We can send as many people as can fit inside the circle. Anyway, it will be five passengers, not four."

"What do you mean?" I asked.

"I'll be coming too," Victoria said.

"Oh?" I asked, a little confused. "Don't you need to cast the spell?" When they'd sent Leon and me to Bodmin Moor, both witches had been chanting the words of the spell, each chanting in a different language.

"The spell does need to be cast by two witches," Devon said, "but we think one of the witches can be in the circle."

"You think? You mean you don't know?"

"Alec, don't worry, everything will be fine," Victoria said in a soothing tone. "Now, let's get on with it."

As we walked through the empty shop to the room at the back, she said, "As I told you on the phone, Devon and I sometimes use faerie magic and invoke the name of the Lady of the Forest when we cast our spells. Faerie magic is rare; there aren't many spell books around that deal with it. So, I thought that if I helped you rescue the Lady of the Forest…" She trailed off, not needing to finish her sentence.

"She'll give you a secret faerie spell or something in return," I said.

"Well, I'm sure she'll be grateful. And if I mention that I'm a practitioner of the art, then maybe she'll share a little something with me."

I shrugged. "Maybe. Anyway, you're welcome to join us. The more of us there are, the better our chances."

We got to the room where the magic circle and the altar were set up. The smell of marigolds and hawthorn berries hung in the air, emanating from the smoking cauldron on the altar. Devon passed around the silver bowl from the altar and five daggers and we all put a drop of blood into the bowl.

Devon returned to the altar and began to chant. Victoria, who was standing next to me, also began to chant in a language different to the one Devon was speaking. As before, the words seemed to deflect off each other and echo around the room, as if the two languages we warring with each other.

The energy in the room became electric, as if lightning were revolving around the circle's edge at an ever-increasing speed.

Then, both witches spoke words that—despite the different languages—seemed to mingle and fuse together. When that happened, Devon poured the contents of the silver bowl into the cauldron and smoke became blood red.

The room around us vanished and was replaced with the ruined stone walls of a church. There was no roof and the blue sky above us was stained orange from the rising sun. The air tasted salty and I could hear the sea crashing against rocks somewhere beyond the ruined church.

Victoria was beaming. "Welcome to the island of Dia. I believe that is the Mediterranean Sea we can hear in the background."

"Great job," I said. Then a thought struck me. "How are you going to get us home if you both have to chant the spell and you're halfway across the world from each other?"

She dug into the pocket of her black lace dress and produced a cellphone. "We'll cast the spell together over

ADAM J. WRIGHT

the phone. We may be witches, dear, but we aren't Luddites."

A second thought struck me but I didn't voice it. What if we lost Victoria in the battle ahead? How would those of us who were left get home?

That led to a third thought that there might not be *any* of us left. I pushed that thought away and tried to stop thinking.

Instead, I went to a place where a section of the stone wall was missing and looked out at the island of Dia.

The ruined church was surrounded by the ruin of what had once been a village but all that was left of the place now were wind-eroded walls and scatterings of rubble. The village was situated at the northern tip of the island.

To the south, an old ruined road led to the southern tip of the island where the mansion we'd seen on the Internet sat looking out over the deep blue Mediterranean Sea. The dawn light picked out other islands in the heat-hazed distance.

The landscape between here and the mansion was a flat, rocky wasteland, the only area of interest a harbor situated halfway between the village and the house. Two small yachts were docked there, probably the only means of getting on and off the island other than by magic.

The sun was rising above the eastern horizon, casting its light over the island. If we could free our friends and get them out of the mansion, the vamps wouldn't be able to follow us. That should give Victoria and Devon time to cast the spell to get us out of here.

Of course, we'd still have to deal with any demons on the island because the sunlight didn't affect them. But at least Korax and Damalis would be taken out of the equation.

I looked at my band of adventurers and figured we might just have a chance to pull this off.

Felicity and Leon were armed with swords and I knew they were both capable of using them.

I reminded myself to put more time into training Felicity in armed combat. Because she was so skilled at research, I tended to use her more in that capacity than as a fighter but that should probably change. As she had said, if she was going to become an investigator, she needed to be expert in all aspects of the job.

Michael was armed with a shotgun. The cartridges contained fragments of wood as well as the usual steel shot. The ex-military man was an expert in the use of the firearm, as I'd seen on a number of occasions.

Victoria looked the most unassuming, dressed in her retro black dress and carrying no weapon at all. I knew that despite her appearance, she had a lot of magical power. She and her sister had managed to close down a gate that would have let a pantheon of dark gods into the world.

I didn't know how well Victoria would operate without her sister around but I had no reason to doubt her solo abilities.

There was a look of grim determination in everyone's eyes. I trusted these people with my life and I knew they trusted me with theirs. I told myself that I must not let them down.

"Everyone ready?" I asked them.

When they all nodded in reply, I said, "Okay, let's go."

We moved south along the rubble-strewn road as the sun rose higher in the sky and bathed us in its light.

CHAPTER 28

WHEN WE REACHED THE MANSION, I was surprised to find that it was modern. Built of stone with huge windows, it had three levels above ground and, I guessed, more beneath. No self-respecting vampire lived in a house that didn't have a basement, and most lairs had a dungeon.

We met no resistance on our way to the house from the ruined village and that was probably because the vamps didn't expect intruders on the island. The place was feared and avoided by the locals.

Up close, it was easy to see the metal shutters behind the windows. They were closed tight, keeping out the sun. Maybe we could open them and increase our chances against the vamps.

The house was accessed by a set of heavy-looking wooden double doors carved with an intricate pattern of letters and symbols.

"Shall we see if it's locked?" I said, stepping forward.

"Wait," Victoria said. "It's warded." She closed her eyes and muttered a few unintelligible words before pointing both hands at the door. Green sparks ran around the carved patterns for a couple of seconds before sputtering out. "It's safe to enter now," she said.

The door handles were two large steel rings. I grabbed one, turned it, and pushed. The door opened with a slight creak. The square of light that shone through the open doorway illuminated a marble floor but nothing else. Darkness shrouded the interior of the house.

There was a slight smell of sulfur hanging in the air. "Watch out for demons," I whispered, stepping inside and unsheathing my sword. Leon and Felicity did the same. The enchanted glow cut through the darkness and lit up the foyer around us.

There were no furnishings, simply a large marble staircase that led up to the next level.

"Should we go up?" Leon whispered.

I shook my head. "Vampires are usually traditionalists. If they have prisoners, they'll be holding them in a dungeon beneath the house." I pointed at a closed wooden door that led farther into the house on this level. "Let's try through there."

We made our way across the foyer slowly and carefully, expecting an attack at any second. The fact that we'd made it this far without meeting any opposition made me wonder if the demons and vampires were lying in wait somewhere within the house, ready to spring a trap on us.

I opened the door and stepped back, ready to fight whatever came rushing at me from the other side.

But the room beyond was as quiet as the grave.

I stepped through the doorway into a lavishly furnished library. Every wall was covered with bookshelves. There were reading lamps set on side tables next to plush leather armchairs. The lights were all off at the moment and our glowing swords were the only illumination. The library was so large that the corners of the room were hidden in shadow.

A door in the opposite wall was the only way out of the room except for the door we 'd entered by. I figured that if we were going to find a door to the basement, dungeon, or whatever was beneath the ground level, we'd find it in the kitchen or one of the rooms at the back of the house and that door seemed to lead in that direction.

I went ahead and opened it slowly. The room beyond the door was pitch black so I thrust my sword forward to cast some light in there. The blue glow showed what looked like a large ballroom. The wooden floor was polished to a smooth sheen, displaying a floral pattern made of darker wood in its center.

The ceiling was arched and decorated with reliefs of vines and flowers. Crystal chandeliers hung over the dance floor. The walls were hung with paintings of people dressed in costumes from various historical periods. There were six windows in this room but all had been shuttered.

I went over the nearest shutters and looked for a way to open them. But the heavy metal sheets were bolted into place, so it looked like they couldn't be opened at all, even at night.

"Damn it," I said. "If we could open these, we'd have a better chance of survival."

Victoria stepped forward and examined the shutters closest to her. "I can open them with magic but it will be very noisy. Loud enough to wake the dead."

I considered that. We'd made it this far without being discovered. If the vampires were sleeping somewhere in the house, I'd rather not wake them. The element of surprise might be our only advantage and I didn't want to waste it.

"We'll keep quiet for now," I told Victoria.

She nodded in understanding. "Of course. You just tell me when you want them to be opened and I'll do it right away."

A number of doors led from the ballroom. I went for the one that led in the same direction we'd been moving since we'd entered the house and opened it to find a dark dining room furnished with a long table, stone fireplace, and more paintings and shuttered windows on the walls.

The next room was a kitchen that could have come straight out of the eighteenth-century. A large stone fireplace dominated one wall, cooking pots hanging within it. The fire was dead at the moment. I tried not to think of what might be cooked in those pots when the fire was burning.

"It's as if the house gets older the deeper we go," Felicity said. "The entrance was modern, the library a little less so, the ballroom and dining room more antiquated, and now this."

"So let's hope our next stop will be the medieval dungeon where we'll find our friends," I said, opening a door that revealed stone steps leading down into darkness. "Yeah, I think it's this way."

I followed the steps down, followed by the others. The air turned cold and the smell of damp and decay rose up from below. When we reached the bottom, I estimated that we'd descended thirty or forty feet beneath the house, into the bowels of the island.

Torches set in iron sconces on the walls provided light. There were two passageways; one that led straight ahead and a side passage that led to our left.

"We could split up," Leon suggested.

"We're not going to split up," I said. "We'll go straight ahead. If we don't find Gloria and the others that way, we'll come back here and take the other passage."

We moved forward as one, past side rooms that had been cut out of the rock. The rooms were empty so they held no interest to us. The passage terminated at an open archway. I stopped and signaled the others to do the same.

The room beyond the archway was lit by torches and in their guttering light, I could see three coffins, each lying within a crypt cut into the rock wall. One of the coffins was open, its lid lying on the floor in front of the crypt. I assumed that one belonged to Davos, who would never be returning here. The lids of the other two coffins were closed.

If Korax and Damalis were asleep inside, we could end this here and now by destroying them. Once they were out of the picture, we could search for our friends and only have to worry about any demon minions that were in the house.

The problem was that we'd have to open the coffins to deliver the kind of attack that destroyed a vampire. A stake through the heart had to be accurate; we couldn't just thrust a stake through the side of a coffin and hope for the best.

Cutting off the vampires' heads would be next to impossible without opening the coffins first, and as soon as we removed the coffins from the crypts, the vampires inside would wake up.

I slowly backed away down the passage. I wanted to strike now and take out the enemy but our friends were somewhere in this dungeon and we'd let them down if we got ourselves killed and weren't able to save them just because we made a rash decision.

We went quietly back to the point where a second passage led to the left.

"Man, we should have taken them out while they were sleeping," Leon said.

"We can't risk it," I told him. "We're here to rescue our friends and get out of here. Gloria said that when she has her torc, she can defend her forest from the Cabal. That's all that matters right now."

I set off along the second passageway, certain now that this was where we'd find Jim and the others.

We came to a wide set of steps that took us down to a locked iron gate. Beyond the gate, I could see a passageway lined with cells. I couldn't see who—if anyone—was inside the cells but I did see movement in the shadows at the far end of the passageway.

"Victoria, can you deal with this gate?" I asked.

"I can but it will be noisy."

"That's fine. The time for stealth is over." I could see the figure at the far end of the passageway more clearly now. It was a demon holding a sword and peering at us as if it wasn't sure who we were. Once it realized we were enemies, it would raise the alarm, attack us, or attack the prisoners. We had to get in there as quickly as possible.

Victoria spread her hands toward the gate and mumbled something under her breath. The gate buckled, pulling against the bolts that fastened it to the walls. It toppled forward and crashed onto the stone floor.

The demon rushed toward us, brandishing its sword. When it reached me, it swung its blade overhead, trying to finish me with one swift strike. I dropped to one knee and raised my sword above my head, blocking the attack. The sound of metal clanging against metal echoed off the stone walls.

The demon stepped back, preparing to strike again. I thrust my sword forward into its belly, feeling the enchanted steel slice through skin, muscle, and bone.

The demon's eyes went wide. It dropped its sword and went limp. I angled my blade so that the creature's body slid off it with the help of gravity. The black blood that oozed from the corpse bubbled as it touched the stone floor.

"Alec!" Jim's voice came from a cell to my right. I went over the bars and peered in. "You okay? Where are the others?"

"Everyone's here," he said, "except Gloria. The keys are over there on that table." He pointed at a small table set against the wall where the demon had been standing.

Michael, who was closest to the table, grabbed the keys and began opening cells.

When Detective Frasier was released, she came over to me and said, "I'm worried about Gloria. The vampires took her away."

"They've been taking her away and torturing her regularly," Girard added. "But the last time they took her, they didn't bring her back."

I swore an oath to myself that if Korax and Damalis had killed the faerie queen, I'd make them pay. I wasn't Gloria's biggest fan but she didn't deserve to be killed at the hands of sadistic vampires just so they could take over her forest.

"We'll find her," I said. "The vampires are asleep right now, so they must have her confined somewhere in the upper levels of the house."

"They aren't asleep," Jim said. "They were talking about somebody important coming her today, somebody high up in the Midnight Cabal. There's no way they're sleeping."

I cursed myself for not checking the closed coffins.

"Gloria told them where the torc was hidden," Jim said. "Davos went to get it. He never came back. They don't know what happened to him but they know Gloria told you where the torc is and they assume you have it. Because of their failure to get it, someone from the Cabal is coming here to take over. The vamps can't decide whether to take orders from the newcomer or rebel against the Cabal."

"Hopefully, we'll be long gone by the time they decide," I said. "If there's someone high up in the Cabal ranks coming here, we don't want to stay and introduce ourselves."

"So let's find Gloria and get the hell out of here," Frasier said.

We made our way back along the passage to the ruined gate. "Are you guys okay?" I asked. "Did they torture you too?"

"No, they left us alone," Jim said. "They were only interested in Gloria. I think they were just going to kill us eventually, probably serve us up as dinner for their esteemed guest."

We ascended the two sets of steps that took us to the kitchen. The house was still quiet. If someone important was coming here, it didn't make sense that there was no activity, no sign of life.

I guessed the others were thinking the same thing because as we moved through the dining room, we were all silent, lost in our own thoughts. I was glad we'd found Jim, Frasier, and Girard alive and well but I was wondering if our enemies had let us into the house, if they'd set a trap for us.

Maybe they thought we were foolish enough to bring the torc here and they hoped to take it from us. The older vampires I'd dealt with in the past had a sense of arrogance that sometimes made them underestimate everyone around them.

The vamps I was dealing with here were far older than any I'd encountered before so their egos were probably off the charts. That could work in our favor if they underestimated us enough to let us get the drop on them.

I opened the door that led to the ballroom and stepped back when I noticed the lights were on in there. The room was bright beneath the glow of the crystal chandeliers. I saw figures in there, at the far end of the room.

"Come in," said a male voice that sounded as cold as a cemetery breeze.

CHAPTER 29

I STEPPED FORWARD INTO THE ballroom, my fingers tightly clenched around my sword's grip. At the other end of the room stood the two vampires I assumed to be Korax and Damalis.

Korax was similar to Davos in appearance with long straight black hair that reached beneath his shoulders but he wore a loose white poet's shirt with lace at the cuffs, dark breeches, and high black boots.

Damalis wore a long red and black dress that plunged low in the front to display her ample cleavage. Her long black hair was piled on top of her head. Her eyes were dark and cruel and when they looked at me, I looked away.

On the floor between them was Gloria. She had no visible injuries at all but she lay on the floor with her eyes closed, looking as if all the life force had been drained from her. At least I could see she was still breathing; her chest rose and fell slowly beneath her green-check shirt.

"What have you done to her?" I asked through gritted teeth.

It was Damalis who answered. She sneered, showing me her fangs, and said, "You don't come into our house and demand answers from us. We demand them of you. Where is Davos? And where is the torc that belongs to this creature?" She indicated Gloria with a dismissive wave of her hand.

They didn't know I'd killed Davos. Their arrogance probably wouldn't let them even entertain that idea.

"Come closer, all of you," Damalis said softly.

"Don't look in her eyes," I warned the others.

We remained where we were, weapons ready. Tension filled the room.

Korax broke the silence. "Where is Davos?" he blurted out. He didn't have the poise or control of Damalis and I knew that when this standoff became a fight, I was going to have to take him out first.

"Korax, control yourself," Damalis told him.

"But they must know where he is," Korax said angrily. "They know where my beloved Davos is." His voice became pitiful. "Why did he not return to us, sister?"

If they thought Davos was still alive—whatever that meant to a vampire—I had an extra card to play in my gamble to get Gloria back. "I know where he is," I said.

"Where?" Korax demanded.

I ignored him and looked at Damalis. "I believe you want to bargain with me. You know what I want: the faerie queen. I know what you want: the torc and the location of Davos. So how are we going to play this?"

"It's quite simple," she said. "You tell us where Davos is and give us the torc or the faerie will die. *That* is how we are going to play this."

"I tire of this," Korax said. "We should torture the information out of them, the same as we did with the faerie."

"Perhaps," Damalis said, "but we will not have time to do that if the Cabal take over this operation. We might never find out where Davos is." She reached down and picked Gloria up by her throat.

The faerie queen was as limp as a rag doll and didn't even struggle. Damalis glared at me. "Tell us what we wish to know now or I will end the life of this faerie."

"Victoria," I said, "lose those shutters."

Victoria nodded and spread her hands, muttering an incantation. The shutters twisted and ripped themselves from the walls. As they fell from the windows, sunlight streamed into the room.

Damalis and Korax screamed in pain as their flesh blistered and smoked. Damalis dropped Gloria and turned to flee the room. Korax was also running for the door but the pain he was experiencing made him stumble.

Michael fired the shotgun, steel and wood ripping into Korax's body and knocking him off his feet. I rushed forward, ready to strike a killing blow and cut off the vampire's head. He was scuttling along the floor on all fours like a spider, his speed superhuman despite the weakening effects of the sunlight on his body.

Damalis had already gone through the door to the library and I thought Korax would make it there before I reached him but just as he got to the open door, it closed in his face. Damalis obviously valued her own safety over that of her brother.

"Sister," he cried out, "why are you doing this?" He reached up for the door handle but by the time he wrapped his blistered fingers around it, I'd reached him. He turned to face me with wide eyes. "No!"

I swung the sword so hard that it passed through his neck and dug into the wood of the door so deeply that I had to brace my boot against the door to pull the blade free.

Korax's head and body burst into flames. I stepped over them and went to Gloria, crouching down beside her and cradling her head in my arm. "Gloria, can you hear me?"

Her eyes opened slowly and she looked up at me with a weak smile. "Alec, you came to rescue me. My hero."

"I'm going to get you out of here." I handed my sword to Jim, slid my arm beneath Gloria's knees and lifted her up.

She put her arms around my neck. "I think it may be too late for that. The vampires burned me with iron until I told them where the torc was. It was too much for me. I'm mortally wounded."

I wasn't sure if she was being serious or overly dramatic. She looked fine. "I can't see a scratch on you."

"Of course you can't. My appearance is a glamor. It isn't real. You should leave me here, Alec, because I'm dying. I'll only slow you down."

"I'm getting you out of here," I told her again. I looked at the others. "We need to get back to the village. Look out for Damalis; she's been hurt but she may have some fight left in her."

Leon and Michael led the way through the door to the library. Felicity hung back with me, a concerned look on her face as she kept glancing at Gloria in my arms. She obviously believed the faerie was dying. I was beginning to believe it too; Gloria telling me to leave her here had been more than just a dramatic gesture.

Frasier and Girard stayed close behind me and Jim and Victoria took up the rear as we passed through the library and then into the marbled foyer. There was no sign of Damalis. She was probably hiding somewhere upstairs, licking her wounds. I just hoped we could get out of here before she recovered enough strength to attack us.

Leon opened the door that led outside and went out with Michael to make sure our escape route was clear. He came back inside a moment later. "We may have a problem. There's a boat in the harbor that wasn't there before."

"You see anyone on it?"

"No."

I turned to Victoria. "Call Devon and get ready to cast that spell as soon as we get to the church."

She nodded and took her phone from the pocket of her dress.

We left the house and began to move north across the rocky waste ground toward the village. I could see the boat Leon had mentioned, a luxury yacht tied next to two smaller ones we'd seen earlier.

"It looks like the high-ranking Cabal member has arrived," I said to Felicity.

"Yes, but I can't see anyone on board. Perhaps they know there's a problem so they're not coming ashore."

"Let's hope it stays that way," I said.

I should have known it was too good to be true. Less than a minute later, the yacht burst into life. Figures swarmed over the decks and onto the dock. They weren't preternatural creatures, just normal-looking men and women dressed in black combat gear and carrying guns. They began running up from the harbor toward the village.

I broke into a run, glad that Gloria was a lightweight. "Victoria, get that spell going," I said. "We haven't got a minute to spare."

She gave me the thumbs up, running with her phone pressed to her ear as she spoke to her sister.

"I could hold them off, sir," Michael offered, brandishing his shotgun.

"No, we're all getting out of here," I said. "Those soldiers are probably the security detail for whoever is on that boat. I have a feeling those guns aren't just for show."

As we ran, I estimated that we would reach the church before the black-clad army but only by a few seconds. We might have to try to hold them off after all while Victoria and Devon got the spell working.

The trouble was, we were armed for vampires and demons, not humans with assault rifles. We'd brought swords to a gunfight and we might end up paying for it with our lives.

When we finally reached the ruined village, Gloria looked at me with tired eyes and said, "Alec, I'm not going to make it."

"Just hold on a little longer," I told her.

We ran into the church ruins and gathered together while Victoria began reciting the spell. I could faintly hear Devon on the other end of the phone doing the same.

The armed members of the group—Jim, Leon, Felicity, and Michael—formed a protective circle around Victoria, Gloria, and me. I could hear the boots of the Cabal security force pounding on the ground outside the walls.

Then, suddenly, they swarmed into the church and surrounded us, rifles held at shoulder height, red laser sights steady. Now that I could see them closer, I could see a red magic circle emblem on the left breast of their combat jackets. I'd never seen it before but I assumed it was the symbol of the Midnight Cabal.

274

They kept their distance, simply pointing their weapons at us. It was a standoff, except we were outgunned and had no hope of surviving if they pulled their triggers.

Victoria and Devon continued to work the spell. The air became charged with magic.

I didn't understand why the soldiers were letting us continue the spell. If they were members of the Midnight Cabal, why weren't they shooting? A vortex of energy began to swirl around us and the soldiers stepped back slightly.

The soldiers near the gap in the wall parted to let a woman through. Unlike the others, she was dressed in white—white pants and a white sweater with the same magic circle emblem on the left breast but fashioned into a gold pin.

She walked up to the edge of the swirling magical vortex and looked at me.

When I saw her familiar brown eyes, I knew who she was immediately. My mind tried to reject the information at first, telling me this woman couldn't possible be who I thought she was. I must be mistaken. But the doubt crumbled when she said, "Alec."

That voice was etched in my memory. The last time I'd heard it was in a car eighteen years ago. I'd been nine years old at the time and it had been the last time I'd seen my mother.

"Mom?" I said.

"Alec, I—"

Whatever she said next was lost to me. My mother and the soldiers disappeared and I was standing in the magic circle at Blackwell Books, Gloria in my arms, my friends standing with me.

I felt numb inside. All this time I'd thought my mom was dead, she'd been part of the Midnight Cabal. Why hadn't she tried to contact me? Why had she chosen not to be a part of my life?

Gloria reached up and touched my cheek. She smiled weakly, a tear running down her cheek. "Alec, thank you for coming to save me." The touch of her fingers felt like soft petals against my skin. Then I realized her fingers actually were petals.

Her hand had changed, becoming a mass of white flowers. The flowers spread down over her arm, onto her shoulder.

"Gloria, what's happening?"

"It's okay," she whispered gently.

She closed her eyes, relaxed in my arms, and died, her body turning into white orchids, lilies, roses, and daisies. They tumbled over my arms and onto the floor until I was holding nothing and all that was left of the faerie queen was a pile of flowers at my feet.

"Oh my God," Felicity said, stepping away from the flowers. She removed her glasses and wiped tears from her eyes.

The room became silent as everyone looked down at the mass of white flowers on the floor.

276

I'd failed the Lady of the Forest. Failed to protect her. Failed to help her get her land back. Some hero I turned out to be.

I left the room, feeling guilt and anger warring within me. I swore an oath to myself that the Midnight Cabal was going to pay for this. In their eagerness to defeat the Society, they'd steamrolled over everything in their path, not caring who got hurt.

I felt a hand on my shoulder and turned to face Felicity.

"Alec, don't blame yourself for this."

"I'm going to make them pay, Felicity. I'm going to show them that they can't just destroy whatever stands in their way."

"That woman at the church. You called her—"

"It was my mother. I don't understand how or why but she's obviously part of the Cabal."

She nodded slowly, thinking through the implications of that in her mind.

"Do you think your father found out she was still alive and that has something to do with his disappearance?"

"I have no idea. All I know is that I'm going to stop the Cabal, no matter who its members are."

CHAPTER 30

We all stood around a low table in the Blackwell Books reading area. The sisters obviously didn't mind people coming into the shop and reading books for free because they'd arranged a table and armchairs for just that purpose. There was even a coffee machine sitting on an antique credenza.

They'd collected the flowers from the floor of the back room and placed them in a silver bowl, insisting that we all drink a toast to the faerie queen. I'd gone out to the Land Rover and retrieved the torc, putting it on the table next to the bowl.

Frasier had called her family, telling them that she was coming home soon. I wasn't sure what story she was going to tell them to explain her absence.

Felicity had spoken to her mother on the phone, saying she was still in Exeter and would be home later today.

Devon and Victoria were standing at the credenza, fussing with wine glasses and a bottle of something dark that I hoped they hadn't concocted themselves. Their herbal teas were bad enough; I wasn't sure I could drink something they'd made with alcohol and live to tell the tale.

When they turned and handed out the full glasses, Victoria said, "Here we are, a nice glass of sherry for everyone. I'm afraid we only keep store-bought liquor in the shop. We keep the good stuff at home."

"Don't worry about it, this will be just fine" I said, accepting a glass and reminding myself to never go to the witches' home for a drink.

Devon stood by the bowl of flowers and raised her glass. "To the Lady of the Forest. May her spirit return to the land of eternal summer." We drank. The sherry was sweet and strong.

"Now, to the matter of getting everyone home," Victoria said. "We'll send the Canadians first, I think, then Felicity can be on her way back to England. Is that okay with everyone?"

There were murmurs and nods of assent.

"I'll be going back to England too," I said. "Just for a short trip. There's something I have to do."

CHAPTER 31

Wʜᴇɴ ᴡᴇ'ᴅ ᴀʟʟ ᴅʀᴀɪɴᴇᴅ ᴏᴜʀ glasses and the witches had gone to the back room to make preparations, Jim, Frasier, and Girard came over to me.

"Thank you for making sure we got home safely," Frasier said. "My husband and kids would thank you too but I'm not sure what I'm going to tell them about all this. I'm still trying to process it myself."

"You'll think of something," I said.

Girard shook my hand, his grip strong. "I don't know what to say. I was an ass."

"Yes, you were," I said, grinning.

"Well, I won't be closing my eyes to what's really going on anymore," he said. "The next murder case that comes across my desk, I'm going to say to myself, "Was this done by humans, trolls, or God-knows-what?" Maybe I'll close more cases that way."

"Maybe you will."

"Alec," Jim said, "if you need any help taking on the Cabal, call me. Call me anyway and we can have a beer out back of my house sometime, hopefully without the demon party-crashers."

"Sounds good," I said. "Take care of yourself, Jim. At least you have two members of the force who will be only too willing to help the next time you get stuck on a case."

"Stuck?" he asked, eyeing me suspiciously.

"Well, you did call me because you couldn't figure out those murders."

"No, I called you because my dreams were being manipulated. Otherwise, I'd have solved everything on my own."

"You keep telling yourself that."

He wrapped his huge arms around me and hugged me. "It was good to see you again."

"You too," I said when he released me from the bear hug and I could breathe again.

They went to the back room. I assumed the witches would send them to a church in Huntsville. I just hoped there wouldn't be anyone in the church when Jim, Frasier, and Girard appeared out of nowhere.

"Hey, Alec," Leon said, "Michael and I are going to head home. Call me if you want to hang out or drive the Porsche or something."

"I will. Thanks for your help."

"And definitely call me if you need any demons killed or vampires slain."

"Preferably when I've finished my holiday, sir," Michael added.

I laughed. "Okay, I'll keep that in mind."

They left. I turned to Felicity. "Thanks for helping me out,"

"You don't have to thank me, Alec. It's my job."

"I know but I pulled you away from your father while you were supposed to be looking after him."

"He's doing really well. I don't think he really needs me there anymore."

"That's good."

She nodded and then took a deep breath as if she were about to say something she'd wanted to say for a while. "I'd like to stay there a bit longer if it's all right with you."

"Of course that's all right. Take all the time you need."

"I just need to straighten things out in my mind. A lot has happened recently and I don't want to go rushing headlong into anything while I'm still dealing with things from the past."

"Are you talking about us?" I wasn't even sure what "us" meant' we'd shared a couple of kisses and intimate moments but it hadn't progressed beyond that.

She nodded. "I know I said this before and then I changed my mind. I feel so stupid."

I placed my hands gently on her shoulders. "You shouldn't feel stupid for telling me how you feel. It's fine. And you're free to spend as much time with your parents as you want. Just don't feel like you have to stay over there to avoid me, okay?"

She nodded. "Okay."

"And make sure you're on call when I want you to research something for me."

She smiled. "Of course. Speaking of research, I may have found a cure for Mallory's curse. I need to look into it some more but it seems that the curse could be lifted if Mallory puts the heart from the Box of Midnight into the mummy of the sorceress, Tia."

"That's great news."

"It is and it isn't. We don't know where the mummy is or even if it exists. As I said, I have to look into it some more."

"But it's a start," I said. I didn't add that we also didn't know where Mallory was. I was sure she'd get in contact with me eventually.

Victoria poked her head out of the back room. "Are you two ready?"

CHAPTER 32

WHEN FELICITY AND I ARRIVED in the stone circle at Bodmin Moor, it was early morning, local time. The sky was dull gray and a thin mist hung over the moor. I had the bowl of flowers in my arm, the torc in my hand.

I'd considered returning Gloria to her forest in Faerie but had been told by the witches that now the Lady of the Forest was dead, her part of Faerie would wither and die and become dead ground.

So I would return Gloria's remains and her torc to Vivian, the Lady of the Lake.

Now that Gloria was dead, the torc would slowly die too, losing its power until it became nothing more than a piece of gold jewelry. Until that time, the Lady of the Lake could keep it safe.

"It's cold," Felicity said, hugging herself.

"I'm surprised the Blackwell sisters didn't give you one of their sweaters," I said, grinning. We left the stones and walked along the dirt path to where the Volvo was parked. I held the door open for her and Felicity got in.

I got in the passenger side and we drove to Dozmary Pool. When we arrived there fifteen minutes later, I said, "You should head for Sussex. I can handle this."

"Are you sure? You'll have to walk all the way back to the stone circle."

I nodded. "Yeah, I think this is something I should do alone."

"Alec, you're not responsible for her death."

"I feel responsible." I opened my door and climbed out of the car. "Safe journey. Text me when you get to your parents' place so I know you arrived safely."

"I will. I'll look into that cure too. And perhaps you'd like me to see if I can find out anything more about the Midnight Cabal."

"Yeah, that'd be great." I closed the door. After giving me a quick wave through the window, Felicity set off along the road.

I stood and watched the Volvo disappear into the mist.

Then I turned and walked to the lake.

When I got to the edge of the water, I looked out over the pool. The water was calm, reflecting the gray sky and clouds.

I had no idea if Vivian knew her sister was dead or not; faerie communication was a mystery to me. Maybe the

285

Lady of the Lake had no idea the Lady of the Forest was dead. Or maybe she'd felt a disturbance in the Force or something.

I set the bowl of flowers on the ground and, holding the torc in my hand, said, "I failed you. And I failed your sister. I told you I was going to get the torc to her and help her get her forest back but it didn't work out that way. So I'm returning this to you."

I flung the torc out into the lake. It splashed into the water. I picked up the bowl. "The vampires that were holding your sister captive tortured her until she perished. I brought her remains here so she can be with you." I took a handful of the white flowers and scattered them onto the lake, followed by another and another until every last petal was floating on the still water.

"I'm sorry I couldn't save your sister," I said. "But I swear to you that I will avenge her death. The group responsible is called the Midnight Cabal and they are my sworn enemies." I remembered my mother wearing the pin that declared her allegiance to the Cabal and added, "Every last one of them."

The lake was silent. I watched the flowers floating on the water's surface for a moment before deciding it was time to make the walk back to the stone circle and then go home.

I hadn't expected a reply from Vivian; I'd simply come here to do what I thought was right. The torc had been returned; the Lady of the Forest's remains laid to rest with her sister.

I took one last look at Dozmary Pool and turned way, ready to trudge over the misty moor.

A noise from the center of the lake caught my attention. I turned to see the chainmail-clad arm of the Lady of the Lake thrust from the water, as it had been when she'd given me the torc.

But this time, her hand clutched the grip of a sword.

When I saw the weapon pointing at the sky, my pulse began to race. Its blade glimmered even in the dull morning light.

It was of simple design but I immediately knew what it must be; the sword I'd read about as a child, the weapon that had been wielded by King Arthur when he led his knights of the round table on their quest to vanquish evil.

Excalibur.

AFTERWORD

If you want to be informed about new releases in this series, join the Harbinger P.I. Mailing List: http://eepurl.com/bRehez

To contact the author, please use the following email address: adamjwright.author@gmail.com

Thanks for reading!

CPSIA information can be obtained
at www.ICGtesting.com
Printed in the USA
BVHW032145040419
544704BV00001B/9/P

9 781539 775966